BEYOND
THE
WATERFALL

Elaine Breault Hammond

RAGWEED
THE ISLAND PUBLISHER

In memory of my father, Orval Preston Breault,
who, as a boy, read books while herding cattle on the prairie.

Edited by:
Jennifer Glossop
Cover and book illustration by:
Mary Montgomery
Printed and bound in Canada by:
Webcom

Ragweed Press acknowledges the generous support of
The Canada Council for the Arts.

Published by:
Ragweed Press
P.O. Box 2023
Charlottetown, PEI
Canada   C1A 7N7

Canadian Cataloguing in Publication Data

Hammond, Elaine Breault, 1937–
    Beyond the waterfall.
    ISBN 0-921556-68-3
I. Title.
PS8565.A566B49 1997   jC813'.54   C97-950165-2
PZ.H1845Be 1997

Contents

Chapter One

A Picnic
in the Country

"Maggie, I think you're holding out on me!" Colleen said in a tense voice, her fist clenching and unclenching as she spoke.

"I don't know what you're talking about," Maggie answered, but she couldn't look Colleen in the eye.

They were sitting on the grassy bank beside the Saint John River. Sunlight sparkled on the water as the wide, placid river flowed lazily between green wooded hills. Maggie wished she could enjoy the serenity of the day, but she was upset by Colleen's accusation.

Ever since Maggie's holiday on Prince Edward Island last year, Colleen had suspected Maggie wasn't taking her into her confidence. Maggie knew Colleen was hurt and bewildered. They had been best friends for years, and Maggie felt sad that she couldn't tell Colleen about that month on PEI. But how could she tell her that she and Marc had travelled back in time and had lived in an Acadian village in the eighteenth century? Maggie had a hard time believing it herself sometimes. She couldn't talk about it with anyone but Marc. Besides, Colleen would think that she had lost her mind. Rather than risk their friendship, Maggie chose not to say anything.

But just a few minutes ago, when Aunt Kate had gone to the car for the lemonade and left them alone, without thinking she had said, "That's what Antonine used to say."

"Antonine? Who's that?" Colleen had asked.

"Oh, somebody I knew once," Maggie answered, looking down at her hands so that her long hair fell forward and hid her face. She bit her lip. Antonine was her friend in the eighteenth century. She still felt close to her and for a moment had forgotten that Colleen didn't know her. That's when Colleen had become upset.

Both girls were quiet as Aunt Kate returned with an insulated jug in her hand.

"Now, have a glass of this nice lemonade," she said. She shook the drink container, and ice cubes clacked. Maggie held the plastic glasses, not looking at Colleen. She was glad, for a change, that her great-aunt liked to dominate every conversation. As long as Aunt Kate was talking, Maggie wouldn't have to deal with Colleen.

But suddenly she realized what Aunt Kate was saying. She was telling Maggie and Colleen that they should go for a hike without her. She would drive them into the forest, and they could hike from the road to a hidden waterfall while she got caught up on her reading.

"I hiked in there many times — when I was much younger, of course. It's a bit rough, but nothing you young people can't handle. I'm too old and my joints are too stiff for that kind of hiking. But I remember the falls as being quite wonderful."

"What a great idea!" Colleen said, leaping to her feet. "What're we waiting for? Let's go."

Maggie looked at the tree-covered hills on the far side of the river. She protested that it was too hot to climb, but, as usual, Aunt Kate wouldn't listen. "I can't think of a better way for young girls to spend a summer afternoon than going for a hike. Now, Maggie, don't argue!"

Maggie glowered, but she followed Colleen to the car. Aunt Kate drove them down a little winding road, with trees crowding its sides. She stopped and pointed to a trail through the trees.

"It should take you about an hour to get there, then an hour to come back. I'll be waiting here for you at" — her voice trailed off as she checked her watch — "at four forty-five. Precisely. That gives you twenty-five minutes to catch your breath at the falls. You'll want to spend a few minutes looking at them, after all."

Colleen and Maggie changed from their shorts into jeans in the back seat of the car. They didn't want to, but Aunt Kate insisted it was better than exposing bare legs to bug bites and scratches from branches. Maggie smoothed her long, dark brown hair back from her face into a ponytail. Colleen pulled a baseball cap on over her short auburn curls.

The path to the waterfall was barely discernible. At first the terrain was uneven and they had to watch their footing, hard to do in heavy undergrowth. Maggie decided to keep ahead of Colleen — if possible, too far ahead for any embarrassing questions. Soon she was breathing heavily, and sweat was dripping from the end of her nose. The air was heavy with the sweet smell of bruised and broken leaves and fronds.

"Hey, wait up!" gasped Colleen.

Maggie kept going.

"Ouch!" Colleen yelled.

Maggie stopped and turned around. Colleen was standing still, her hands over her face.

"What happened? Are you okay?" Maggie asked.

Colleen pulled her hands from her face. There was a faint red line on her cheek. "Just ran into a branch. Let's sit and catch our breath."

"Not yet. Aunt Kate will be keeping track of time. If we're not back when she said, she'll have the Mounties looking for us with dogs or something."

"I didn't think you cared about Aunt Kate's fussing," said Colleen.

"We have twenty-five minutes to look at the falls. Remember?" Maggie grinned. "We can talk then." Maggie knew that was what Colleen wanted — not to rest, as she said, but to ask more questions. Maybe she should tell Colleen everything about her journey back in time. Maybe there was a way to go about it that she hadn't thought of yet. She felt guilty about shutting out her best friend from the most significant experience of her life.

She didn't feel guilty about not telling her adventures to her Aunt Kate. Even though the old lady had been taking care of her since she was six years old, when her mother died, they had never been close. She had a thousand secrets from Aunt Kate. And she believed Aunt Kate liked it that way. She took good care of Maggie out of a sense of duty, but she wasn't really interested in young people. She had no inclination to share confidences.

But Colleen had always been there for her. She'd been her best friend since grade one. While Maggie was short and small-boned, Colleen was tall and slim. Maggie's long brown hair was ordinary-looking, but Colleen's hair was a beautiful red. She was so tall that her halo of auburn curls floated above the crowd of heads at school, and Maggie could always pick her out at assembly.

Neither girl was a joiner. They both liked solitary amusements: sailing, horseback riding and biking. They loved the same books. When Maggie wanted to be alone, she wrote stories and poetry. Colleen spent hours practising the piano. They had always told each other everything — until now.

Maggie ploughed on through the woods. Occasionally she felt the sharp bite of a black fly, but few bugs were active in the heat of the afternoon. Her tee-shirt caught on a branch, and as she impatiently pulled it away, she felt it rip, but she didn't pause. She could feel dribbles of sweat sliding down her ribs. She rubbed her damp hands against her shirt and kept going.

"What's the big hurry? You're acting as if you're running away from something!" Colleen complained. But she was keeping up with Maggie's frenzied pace. She was too competitive to let Maggie get ahead.

The path was still climbing. Maggie grabbed a branch with one hand to pull herself along. Something was compelling her along at breakneck speed. At first she had hurried because she wanted to get away from Colleen's questions. But now something else was making her push her way between branches and find footing amid the undergrowth. She sensed that reaching the waterfall in time was terribly important. She had the strangest feeling that something was waiting for her there.

She could hear Colleen's breath coming in ragged gasps just behind her. Then she heard a thud and a screech. She stopped and whirled around. Colleen had disappeared.

Chapter Two

The Hidden Waterfall

"Colleen!" Maggie screamed.

"Here," Colleen answered. Her voice sounded muffled.

Stunned, Maggie hurried a few steps back down the path. The shrubs looked flattened, but the path was empty.

"Maggie!" Colleen's voice came from the side of the path, but sounded far away.

"Where are you?" Maggie called, but, even as she spoke, she noticed a gap in the bushes. She bent over and peered through. What she saw made her gasp. The path skirted a deep crevice. Colleen had stepped over the edge and fallen. There she was, a couple of metres down the slope, her slide stopped by a rock jutting from the hillside.

Colleen tried to climb the slope on her hands and knees, but it was too steep and she slid back. Maggie lay on her stomach and reached down. Her fingers brushed Colleen's.

With one arm around the trunk of a small tree, she stretched as far as she dared. This time she was able to grasp Colleen's hand and pull as Colleen crawled. In a moment, Colleen was sitting on the path beside her. She looked shaken.

"Are you hurt?" asked Maggie.

"I don't think so," Colleen said, tentatively getting to her feet. She wiggled one arm, then the other, and took a step or two. "Everything seems to work, but my ankle hurts a bit. I think I've had enough hiking for one day. Let's start back to the car."

"No," said Maggie quietly. "Let's keep going. If you're sure you're okay. We're almost there."

Colleen looked incredulous. When she spoke, her voice was shaking. "You didn't even want to come. But now you seem obsessed with getting to that stupid waterfall. What's going on, Maggie?"

"I don't know. I can't explain it. I didn't feel this way when we started hiking, but you're right — now I really *must* get to the waterfall. I'm sorry, Colleen. If you don't want to come with me, you can wait with Aunt Kate at the car. I'll go to the falls on my own. It's something I have to do."

"All right. If you say so," said Colleen, her tone chilly. "I'd probably just slow you down. Go ahead without me." She turned and started back to the car.

"Colleen, don't be like that!" Maggie called after her.

Colleen didn't turn. She kept up her slow pace, her head bowed, perhaps because she was being cautious of her footing, perhaps because she was crying. Finally, she disappeared into a sea of green.

Maggie sighed. In a moment her frustration disappeared in a resurgence of her compulsion to reach the waterfall. She plunged along the path, wary of stepping to the side now that she was aware of the hidden chasm, but hurrying nonetheless. After a few minutes, she stopped to wipe the sweat from her eyes with her shirt. Then she heard it for the first time — the hiss and splash of falling water. It gave her new energy.

She fought her way along the last few metres, then through a tangled screen of bushes. There it was. She was standing near the edge of the chasm that Colleen had nearly fallen into. With no trees in front of her, she had a clear view of a stream of water tumbling over a rocky ledge on the other side of the chasm. The falling water was gossamer-like, plunging into the gorge far below.

It was not a very wide waterfall. It hung in the air like a piece of lace. The sun caught the mist, and a rainbow arced over it.

Maggie hunkered down and watched, soaking in the beauty. For the first time that day, she felt at peace. After a few minutes, she rose and continued following the trail leading to the falls on the other side. As she got closer, she could smell the moisture in the air, and her ears filled with the music of the stream.

Before she reached the falls, the path veered toward the edge of the cliff. Maggie cautiously peered over the precipice. Between shrubs and crooked, stunted trees, a rocky path wound down to the floor of the gorge, very near the foot of the falls.

Without considering the danger, Maggie started down. She stayed low, close to the earthen track, steadying herself with a hand on a rock or grasping a swath of tough grasses or the branches of a shrub, while searching with eyes and feet for her next step. At the bottom, the sound of the falling water was louder, having gathered in the cup of the gorge and concentrated there.

Her sense of purpose was overwhelming. Like a sleepwalker, she walked toward the falls. With the perfume of the mist and the drops of water on her face, she didn't care that her feet were getting wet. She didn't care when she felt her shirt being plastered against her. She didn't flinch at the roaring sound which was all around her now, much louder than she had expected.

She was very close to it before she realized that the path she was following disappeared behind the falls. She didn't hesitate. She followed the path, even though, as she passed into the darkness, it felt as if she was caught in a deluge. The gorge faded from her consciousness, and the world consisted only of water beating against her and noise thundering through her.

In a moment the force passed. She rubbed the water from her face as she regained her perspective. She was standing under a rocky ledge, in a hollow behind the falls. Remarkably, it was dry, like a protected place under a thickly branched tree in a rainstorm. From her dark hollow, she could see streaks of light flashing through the falls from the outside. She had a strong sensation that she was standing outside of the world, looking in, but not able to see much. It was as if, at any moment, she would see everybody in the world going about their business but they couldn't see her. She shivered. It was an eerie feeling, but she liked it. She felt safe, yet, somehow powerful. As if she was meant to be there.

She stared at the falls, waiting for a vision to appear. Then, suddenly, with no warning, the water caught her. She didn't remember moving, but she was in the falls and she was being whirled along, pushed and carried by a force that was somehow familiar. She was flying through water at an incredible speed, but she was not frightened. She knew with a calm certainty that it was for this watery journey that she had been led to the falls.

Chapter Three

Behind the Waterfall

$\mathcal{I}$t was night. Maggie shivered and hugged herself, arms across her chest. Her first thought was that her clothes were dry. The next thing was that, although it was night, she could see clearly. A huge moon hung in the sky and illuminated everything around her with a pale silvery light. She slowly turned around, looking in every direction. Behind her was a dark mass of bushes from which came the gurgle and splash of water. In front of her was an empty plain, stretching as far as she could see in the moonlight.

Maggie hugged herself tighter. She felt an overwhelming sense of loneliness. It was as if no one existed, except her. She had somehow been transported into an empty world.

She was in a field of grass. It wasn't short grass, like a mown lawn. It came halfway up her legs, and when she tentatively took a few steps, it grabbed her sneakers and jeans like fingers clutching and holding her.

She stood still, confused and frightened.

Ooooh, whish. Something fell out of the sky and swooped across her line of vision, rose back to the sky and soared toward the horizon. Maggie raised her arms to shield her face. Between them, she could see the shape of a large bird against the moonlit sky. It was not as close as she had feared. As her eyes followed it, it grew smaller and disappeared. Then, for the first time, she noticed dark shapes against the horizon, several small ones and one larger one. It was as if the bird had been directing her gaze toward them.

She began walking as fast as she could through the long grass. The dark shapes got bigger. In minutes, she could tell she was approaching two buildings. The first one she came to was obviously a small, simple house. Attached to its end wall was a lean-to shed.

When she got close, she could see the large building more clearly. It was several metres away from the first. It had no chimney and at its entrance was a big double door. It was probably a barn with outbuildings nearby.

The house had two dark windows, looking at her like sightless eyes, and between the eyes was a door. Half-frightened but curious, she walked stealthily around the house. The far side had two more windows. She almost ran into a clothesline that stretched from the corner to a skinny tree. Back at the door, she raised her hand to knock, then dropped her hand to her side. It was the middle of the night, she didn't know where she was, and she had no idea what kind of strange people might be sleeping inside, or how angry they might become if they were wakened.

She stood for a moment, not knowing what to do. Gradually a feeling came over her, not unlike the compulsion she had had to reach the falls. This time, something was telling her to go into the house. Nervously she lifted the iron latch. The door swung inward with a little creak, as if someone was pulling it open for her. She stepped across the threshold into a dark room. She pushed the door to close it, but the latch didn't catch and it swung open again, letting moonlight spill across the floor. She cocked her head and listened. Nothing. She took a few steps, then stopped when the floor creaked. Someone coughed, but the sound was muffled and she knew the sleeper was in a different room. She went back and shut the door, then continued across the dim room, oddly not afraid of bumping into furniture, with a sureness of where she was going that she couldn't understand.

There was a partly open door in front of her. She could see a sliver of moonlit window. She pushed gently and, once again, a door swung open as if someone or something was waiting for her. Inside a tiny room, the moonlight beamed down through the single window, illuminating a narrow bed.

Maggie yawned and stretched her arms above her head. She was exquisitely tired. She stretched out on the hard little bed, pulled a blanket over herself and fell asleep.

Chapter Four

A New Land

"Time to get up!" It was a woman's voice from the other side of the door.

Maggie opened her eyes and lay still for a moment, wondering where she was. Suddenly remembering, she shot upright and threw back the blanket. Sunlight streamed in through the little window. It was morning and the people who lived in the house were up and about to discover her. What would they do when they found a strange girl in one of their beds?

She looked down at herself. She had been too exhausted last night to get undressed. She was still wearing her jeans and cotton shirt — even her sneakers! She clawed her long brown hair back from her face, but it was in a snarl, a mess. Then she saw a tiny mirror hanging on the wall, over a shelf on which a black comb sat. As she leaned toward the mirror to comb her hair, her face wavered before her in the murky glass.

Maggie leaned her head back and shut her eyes as she ran the comb through the length of her hair. When she opened her eyes, she noticed a dress hanging from a nail on the wall. She replaced the comb on the shelf and examined the dress. It was made of heavy cotton which had once had a pattern, but it had faded badly and now the material was varied shades of blue-grey, with streaks of blue flowers on a darker blue in the folds of the full skirt. Maggie slipped out of her jeans and tee-shirt and pulled the dress over her head, then she did up the row of flat white buttons that edged the opening from her waist to her neck.

The dress fit perfectly. It was as if it had been made for her! It had long sleeves and a faded blue collar, and it was just long enough to cover her ankles. Her sneakers were poking out from under the skirt, and she realized how ridiculous they looked with this costume. She kicked them off, then pulled off her socks.

Just as she did this, there was a knock on the door and a woman's voice said, urgently, "Ellie, get up! And be smart about it! You don't want to keep Pa waiting."

Maggie froze, her mind racing. So, she was in the room of a girl called Ellie. She felt like an intruder. She looked around, but there was nowhere to hide. The window was only a metre or so from the ground, but she was pretty sure it was too small to climb through. It would be very embarrassing to get stuck, halfway through. Probably the best thing to do would be to face the music. She looked at her clothes lying in a heap on the floor and for a moment thought that she would put them back on; then a second, more insistent, rap came at the door.

Without understanding why she did it, she stuffed her clothes and her watch under the thin mattress. Her sneakers formed a lump, so she pulled them out. Spotting a large rough box in the corner, she lifted the lid and looked down at carefully folded clothing. She slid her hand down the side of the box, feeling the rough wood against her arm, hoisted up the heavy pile of clothes and shoved her sneakers underneath them. Then she ran her hands down her skirt, smoothed her hair back and opened the door.

The first thing she saw was a tall, angular woman busy at an old-fashioned black stove. She had her back to Maggie. Her greying dark hair was pulled to the back of her head in a bun. Maggie could tell by the movement of her arms that the woman was scooping something into a bowl. Then she saw a man sitting at the table, spooning up his breakfast from a steaming bowl. He glanced at Maggie and she froze with apprehension.

"Come sit and get your porridge into you, Ellie, lass," he said. His face was round and shiny, and his grey hair was sparse. He smiled and his eyes crinkled. Maggie began breathing again.

The woman came to the table with a bowl of fried potatoes. "It's near milking time," she said. "I don't know why you're so slow — it's not like you!" She sat down, scolding under her breath. Maggie looked at them both in astonishment. Then, without speaking, she sat. The woman put a bowl of oatmeal in front of her, then passed a pitcher. Maggie poured thick yellow cream on her porridge, sprinkled it with brown sugar and began to eat.

The man and woman were arguing about whether they should dose a sick cow with castor oil or boiled barley. "Lubrication! Lubrication is what she needs," he said.

"Hot mash! Hot mash," the woman repeated steadily in a low voice, speaking sometimes under her breath between mouthfuls of potatoes and bacon.

Maggie was hungry. She ate steadily until her bowl was empty, then the woman plunked down a plate of potatoes and bacon in its place. "Hot mash," she said firmly, looking at the man. Maggie went on eating, glad that the adults were paying so little attention to her. She wondered if they thought she was Ellie only because they hadn't really looked at her.

She also wondered how she had managed to cross the room last night without falling over something. The table was in the middle of the floor, surrounded by dark varnished chairs. Against the whitewashed log walls were the cookstove, a box for wood, a cupboard with two doors on top and two on the bottom, and a small table holding a washbasin and a water pail. Under the table was a slop pail. The board floor was unpainted.

Things were hanging from nails in the walls. Near the stove were two black iron frying pans and a dishpan, near the door were coats and hats, and near the cupboard were cooking utensils. She recognized an eggbeater and a potato masher. Over the door to the outside a gun sat cradled on wooden pegs.

The man, who had started eating first, finished first. He drained the dregs of his tea from the thick white cup and pushed his chair back. When he stood, Maggie could see that he wasn't much taller than she was.

"Time for the barn," he said, waving his hand toward Maggie as he spoke. He was wearing dark pants, a light shirt and a vest. He put on an old felt hat that he pulled down to his ears. With the misshapen hat and his round face, he reminded Maggie of a snowman. He left the house with the words, "Before you come to the barn, Ellie, help Mother put on some mash to boil." As he spoke, a little smile played at the corner of his mouth.

The woman sighed and shook her head, then refilled her cup from a big brown teapot that had lost the tip of the spout. "Better run and catch up with Pa, Ellie. He can't do everything by himself. And neither can I. When you're finished milking, you can help for a couple of hours in the garden. I'll cook the mash. Now, git."

Maggie hesitantly got up from the table. The woman's testy tone made her feel she was being criticized. So far, she hadn't said a word. Now, glancing at the door, then looking down, she said her first words. "My feet?" She was wondering if she should go to the barn with bare feet or go back to the box in the bedroom and dig out her sneakers.

"Your boots are outside. I put them out when I scrubbed the floor last night," said the woman crossly. She rummaged in a clothes basket in the corner, then handed Maggie a pair of clean socks.

Outside the door, in the bright morning light, Maggie slowly pulled on the socks and the pair of dirty workboots with cracks across the toes. She stood for a moment on the unpainted wooden doorstep, looking around her.

Last night she had thought she was on an empty plain, but today she could see sparse clumps of thin trees scattered here and there. Many of the leaves were already yellow. Although the land surrounding her was flat, faraway and dark against the horizon, stood a range of hills. What impressed her most was the sky. In New Brunswick, the sky was the ceiling of the world, with forested hills making high dark walls. Here, in this strange world, the sky was bigger than the earth, seeming to be both ceiling and walls. Fluffy white clouds, looking like castles and forests and sailing-ships, billowed around her. She felt they might scoop her up and sweep her away. Shaking her head as if to awaken herself from a dream, Maggie followed a worn path that linked the house and the barn.

The barn was built of logs, and the roof had grass growing out of it. She stood in the doorway, for the moment not able to see anything in the dimness, but she smelled the warm pungency of animals and she heard rustlings as they chewed their morning food.

She stepped in, out of the sunlight. There were three stalls on either side of the barn, their partitions made of skinny logs peeled of their bark. On one side were six milk cows. One appeared to be sick. Her belly was distended and she stood with her head down, not eating. On the other side was a team of big black workhorses. They nickered and stamped, and shook their heads, as if to greet her, then went back to munching their grain. Two stalls were empty. Some calves in a box stall at the back of the barn were poking their heads through the rails, saying "Maa, Maa," bawling for their breakfast.

The man was milking. When he noticed Maggie in the doorway, he gestured with his head toward a red cow in the next stall. A one-legged milking stool lay on the dirt floor near the cow, and beside it was a metal bucket. Maggie picked up the stool and balanced herself on it, with her forehead against the warm flank of the cow. She positioned the bucket between her knees and began milking. It had been a long time since she had milked a cow, but she hadn't forgotten how. She had helped her Acadian mother milk the family cow, Isabelle, when she had lived in the eighteenth century. The milk sang rhythmically against the side of the pail. It was comforting to rest her head against the warm cow, to listen to the singing of the milk, and to feel the side of the animal moving in and out with its slow, placid breaths. It gave her time to think.

The woman had looked directly into her face when she handed her the socks. Still she had called her Ellie. The man had seen her clearly outlined in sunlight in the door of the barn. He, too, called her Ellie. The clothing in the room she had slept in fit her exactly.

Maggie didn't know who Ellie was. She didn't know whether these people she was living with were good or bad. But she was sure that the force behind the waterfall was like the whirlpool that had spun her back to Old Acadia the previous year. She had no idea where she had been brought this time. She remembered the empty plain in the moonlight. She shivered in spite of the moist warmth of the barn — in part from fear, in part from excitement. When she had left the house, she had seen a calendar hanging from a nail on the wall beside the door. It said September 1894.

Chapter Five

Victoria School

The second morning, after the milking was done, the woman hustled Maggie into Ellie's bedroom. She opened the box by the wall and took out a pink cotton dress with white pearl buttons and a green ribbon at the throat. Maggie slipped out of her faded work dress, then she washed in the cold water in the tin basin on the little table and put on the pretty pink dress. She looked down at it and wished she had a proper mirror so she could admire herself. She took a few dancing steps around the room, until the woman spoke sharply to her.

"Now, now. Don't get to feeling proud of yourself. Remember what the Good Book says about pride going before a fall." Maggie stopped still, her smile fading, confused. The woman pulled the collar straight.

"We made it so many weeks ago, Ellie," she said. "I'm glad we made it a wee bit big, because you've grown this summer."

She left the room, and in a moment was back, holding a length of green ribbon in her hand. "I saved this for the first day at school!"

The woman had a hairbrush in her hand and she began brushing Maggie's long brown hair. She didn't ease up when she hit a tangle, and Maggie winced. Once, when the woman attacked a particularly snarled spot, Maggie yelled, "Ouch!" before she could stop herself. The woman paid no attention. She tied the smooth hair back from Maggie's face with the green ribbon. Maggie looked in the mirror and thought she looked too much like a picture of Alice in Wonderland in an old book Aunt Kate had given her, but she was too polite, as well as a little afraid, to protest.

"Thank you, Mother," she said softly, trying out the name Pa called the woman. Mother didn't smile.

On the way to school, Maggie walked down a rutted trail through the long grass. Earlier, when she had gone to the barn to do the milking, the grass had been white with frost. Pa had said that this was just a taste of worse things to come. Now the sun was getting warm, and the frost had melted.

She picked her way carefully. Of course, she couldn't wear her dirty workboots to school, so she was barefoot. The soles of her feet were tender, and she tried to avoid the sharp grasses and stones.

She could see a small building in the distance and guessed it was the school. There was a flag flying from a pole in front of it. The building across the road from the school was a church; she could tell from the shape of its windows.

While she walked, she considered all her new experiences. She had gone back in time, but not as far back as she had gone last year. Things were old-fashioned, but more modern than in the Acadian village. For one thing, the people here cooked on wood stoves, not in fireplaces. She was happy that everyone spoke English that, except for a few words and expressions, was like the English she usually spoke. This gave her less to worry about. But, where was she? And, even more important, why had she come?

As she approached the school, she could see a boy riding bareback on a white pony dotted with big brown patches. The boy was dressed in dark pants like those Ellie's pa wore. There were three boys of different heights approaching from the west in a wagon pulled by a tired old horse with its head hanging low. A group of smaller children were playing in front of the school, tossing a ball back and forth. She could see all this while still a few minutes from the building because there was nothing on the flat land to block her view.

She was surprised that the unpainted school building was so small. Beyond it were two little structures that she recognized as outdoor toilets, like the one behind the house on the farm. The wagon the three boys were riding in passed the school and pulled up in front of a shed.

As she reached the schoolyard, her steps slowed. She didn't know anyone, but, if she looked so much like Ellie that Ellie's own parents didn't know the difference, these students would not question her. But, she knew kids. They would pounce on any mistake she might make.

She wondered again about this strange magic that made people accept her as one of them. Whatever it was, it put her in a bad position. She wished the magic could prepare her a little better for the people she was supposed to know.

A young woman came to the doorstep of the school and vigorously shook a handbell. At the clang, clang, clang, all the students ran toward her. Maggie counted and, when she joined them, she was the fourteenth. They lined up in two straggly lines — boys and girls. There were ten boys, six of them as big as men, and they jostled and whispered and grinned until the teacher shouted at them.

Maggie was jolted by the teacher's shout. The woman looked rounded and soft, like a little hen, in her plain brown print dress. She had wispy blonde hair and wary eyes that darted from student to student, as if she were fearful that they might do something dreadful at any moment. She had been speaking to the children in a flat, soft voice, but when she told the boys to be quiet, her voice harshened into a surprising shout that seemed quite incongruous. The boys hunched their shoulders under their ears as they stood in an exaggerated version of soldiers at attention. They quit whispering, but they caught each other's eyes and grinned.

Maggie stood behind three others in the girls' line. Two small girls at the front were wearing shoes. The third girl, almost as tall as Maggie, was standing directly in front of her. She was dressed in a print dress that she was growing out of. Her wristbones showed beneath the cuffs, and the skirt came to mid-calf. Her bare feet were caked with dirt.

Once they were all quiet, the teacher spoke once more in her soft inflectionless voice. "Eyes toward the Union Jack." The students' heads lifted as all eyes turned upward to the flag flapping gently in the breeze. Then the teacher began singing "God Save the Queen." Maggie sang along, thankful that this first test of living in the past was no challenge, since she knew the anthem.

Next, the students all folded their hands, bowed their heads and recited the Lord's Prayer. In the middle of the prayer, Maggie felt a sharp pinch on her upper arm. She clutched her arm and gasped with pain. Peeking, she saw one of the big boys smirking.

"Asa!" the teacher growled. Asa laughed under his breath. Maggie moved as far as she dared from the boys' line. "Forward march!" ordered the teacher. Maggie tried to walk as far from Asa as she could, but he was able to give her another painful pinch as they squeezed through the door. The teacher

27

was already inside and didn't see this, but the other boys did and they laughed.

At the front of the room was a black, pot-bellied stove with a long line of stovepipe going up through a hole in the ceiling. There were three rows of wooden desks, each with room for two students sitting side by side. There was a shelf under each desk to hold books. The little children sat at the small front desks, the bigger students at the larger ones at the back. Maggie sat beside the girl with the too-short dress.

"Thank you, Ellie," said the teacher. "Perhaps, with your help, Cora will learn to read this year. I've not had much success teaching Ebenezers anything much." She said this in a scornful tone and Cora hung her head.

The teacher sat at a desk placed on one side of the stove. She pulled open the single drawer and took out a register. A map was hanging on the wall behind her. At the other side of the stovepipe hung a rectangle of blackboard. There were four tall windows along one side of the room. Through them Maggie could see the trail that she had walked that morning, It looked like two black lines that curved and disappeared in the long, waving grass.

On the opposite wall were coat hooks and a shelf where the students had set their lunch pails. At the back of the room was a high bookcase. A few books leaned crazily against each other on the top shelves, but the bottom shelves were empty. Beside the bookcase was a table which held a pail and a tin basin. A dirty towel hung on a nail by the basin.

Maggie listened very carefully when the teacher called the students' names and entered them in the register. Maggie hoped that, if she paid close attention every morning, she would soon learn everyone's name.

Maggie helped Cora practise reading from a small book called a primer which contained simple words for a little child.

Under a pretty white kitten on a blue cushion was written "CAT." Cora could read this. A few pages farther on was the word "WAGON." Cora looked at the picture and said, "Buckboard."

Maggie whispered, "How old are you?" and Cora whispered back that she was ten.

At recess time, the children ran outside. The girls had a small, hard rubber ball to play with. The two little girls, Mary and Rosie, stood side by side, facing Maggie and Cora. Maggie tossed the ball to Rosie, who tried to catch it, her hands cupped in front of her as if waiting to catch handfuls of water. Then Rosie tried throwing the ball to Cora. It fell in the grass at Maggie's feet. All the boys had disappeared into the shed. Maggie wondered what they were doing.

A few minutes later, the teacher rang the bell, then disappeared into the school. The girls ran for the door, but they were not quite fast enough. As she followed the little girls through the door, Maggie heard a cry from behind her. One of the big boys had stepped on Cora's bare foot. Cora limped inside, her face contorted. The big boys were laughing. "Good on you, Bert," Asa said in admiration.

An intense anger swept over Maggie. This boy Asa was even mean to his own sister!

"Quiet!" the teacher barked as they straggled to their seats.

There were arithmetic problems on the blackboard for the older children. The younger ones were told to draw pictures of horses on their slates. The room buzzed with whispers. The teacher paid no attention. She was writing with a long black pen. Every few minutes she dipped the nib in a little bottle of black ink, wiped the nib edges against the side of the bottle and continued writing.

Beside Maggie, Cora pulled her foot onto her knee and rubbed it, wincing. The bottom of her foot was shiny black, and it looked hard, like the sole of a boot.

The big boys took turns going to the water bucket, scooping out water with a tin cup and taking a drink. They poured the remains back into the bucket. When the teacher was not looking, they flicked cold water onto their friends who sat at the back of the room. There were gasps and laughs and muttered threats. In spite of the commotion, the teacher paid no attention.

Finally the long morning came to an end. Maggie got her lunch pail and began eating her sliced pork and pickle sandwiches at her desk. The boys all grabbed their lunch pails and left the room. Cora had only bread spread with a little butter in her lunch pail, so Maggie gave her half a piece of cake.

She knew now where she was. Miss Prentiss had pointed to Manitoba on the map and told the students to memorize the names of the major rivers in their home province. There was no Saskatchewan or Alberta to the west — only a large area marked North-West Territory.

Miss Prentiss folded the papers she'd been writing on all morning and put them into an envelope. Maggie realized now what she had been doing. She had been writing a letter instead of tending to her students!

• • •

That night, in bed, Maggie thought about her first day in this strange new school. It had been horrible. She had a black bruise on her upper arm where Asa had pinched her. She thought of the tears in Cora's eyes when she rubbed her foot where Bert had stepped on it. Although she felt sorry for Cora and had tried to help her, the girl was too shy to say more than a few words. She was too young to be a real friend, anyway.

Maggie hadn't realized until now how much she had been hoping that she had come back in time to be part of a loving family. Since her parents had died when she was small, she'd been well taken care of by her great-aunt Kate and her uncle Jeff. But Aunt Kate cared for her out of a stern sense of duty, not love. And Uncle Jeff had little time for her because of the demands of his business.

Her hopes of a loving family life here in Manitoba seemed futile. Mother acted cross and annoyed all the time. Maggie had no one she could confide in. If she could only get together with Colleen, she was ready to tell her everything. But Colleen might as well be on another planet.

Loneliness washed over her. There was a big aching hollow place in her middle. She curled up in a ball, trying to ease the pain. All she wanted was to escape this bleak place and return home. Tomorrow she would look for the waterfall. She cried herself to sleep.

Chapter Six

Trouble at School

Every day, after school, Maggie changed from her pink school dress into her faded work dress and ran out to the creek to take over from Mother, who was always anxious to get back to the house and her work there. These days Mother had to pickle and preserve the last of the vegetables from her garden before the heavy frosts came. Every day she complained that Maggie must have dawdled on the way home, even though Maggie hurried as fast as she could.

The cows had to be watched while they were grazing to keep them out of the fields, where they might trample and eat the grain. While Mother was watching them, she sat on a blanket sewing and mending, not wasting a moment of important work time. As soon as Maggie appeared, she gathered up her things and hurried off.

While alone with the cows and Rambler, the family's shaggy little dog, Maggie wandered the willows on both sides of the creek, looking for the waterfall. Day after day, she searched, thinking that maybe she hadn't looked in that dark clump or that crack in the bank. She came to think that maybe the falls weren't actually here, but were back in New Brunswick. There might be a passage of some sort, like a hole in the ground, to get back to them. But she could find nothing.

Life on the farm was so busy that it diverted her thoughts from the bitter disappointment of not finding the falls. She could only allow herself a frantic hour of searching each day, then she had to put the falls out of her mind.

She loved the farm animals, and she enjoyed tending the cattle. This task gave her freedom to study her lessons in the golden warmth of late summer days. Whenever a cow strayed into the grain, she called Rambler and he knew exactly what to do. He would circle behind the wandering animal and nip its heels until it returned to the pasture land.

These days Pa was working in the fields with four horses, his team and another team borrowed from a neighbour, all hitched to a big machine called a binder. The binder cut the grain and tied it in bundles called sheaves. Then Pa used a pitchfork to stand several sheaves upright, leaning them against each other for support, so if it rained the water would run away from the precious heads of grain.

There was an air of fearful expectancy, of holding of breath, on the little farm as the family waited for the crop to be threshed. Maggie overheard Pa telling Mother that the unusually heavy rains of the early summer had produced a bountiful crop. When Pa said that the heads were so heavy with grain that they bowed down the stalks, he had a guarded look in his eyes and spoke in a hushed voice, as if he was afraid just speaking about their good fortune might bring on bad luck.

Mother looked sharply at him when he said it was their best crop since they'd taken up their homestead. "Remember that crop that we lost to that hailstorm. And what about the time the grasshoppers ate it all." She shuddered. "I'll never forget how those clouds of grasshoppers darkened the sky and ate up all our profits for the year. No, Pa. Don't count your chickens before they're hatched!"

Life was becoming routine here in Manitoba. Every morning and evening Maggie helped Pa with the chores. The first time he asked her to give their morning oats to the big black work team, Bess and Belle, she had been frightened. She belonged to the Pony Club at home and knew how to ride and groom a horse, but she was used to fine-limbed ponies, not these huge, hairy-footed beasts. But she quickly learned that, in spite of their size, Bess and Belle were gentle and calm. Still, she knew enough to be cautious when caring for them. She guessed that, if ever one accidentally stepped on her foot, she would be lucky if she ever walked again.

Pa made her work with the animals fun. He had names for the milk cows, based on their colour. Maggie smiled when he talked to Blackie, Reddie, Whitie, and Blue, who was a white and black roan that did look a little blue. Having run out of colours, he called the other two Chub and Dora. When she laughed, he laughed with her.

Mother was stern and didn't smile often. She had a saying for every occasion, usually meant to teach Maggie a lesson — and sometimes Pa, too. Although he argued with Mother quite a lot, Pa had great respect for her, and told Maggie to always listen to her mother because she was the one with a head on her shoulders in this family.

It was obvious to Maggie that, somehow, she was taking the place of Pa and Mother's daughter, Ellie. Maggie was very curious about what had happened to the real Ellie, but she couldn't ask anyone since no one realized that anything had happened to her at all.

Maggie told herself not to worry, that when it was time to go back to her own time she would find the falls. In this way, she tried to still the fear nagging at the edge of her consciousness that, this time, she might not get home.

It was breakfast time. The family was seated at the table and Maggie was fuming. She was trying to explain to Pa and Mother why school was so awful. She told about Asa and his constant bullying, and about Miss Prentiss, who didn't seem to care what was happening. Pa was on the school board, so couldn't he do something about it?

"She writes letters and buffs her fingernails and leaves the teaching to me!"

"Now, now, Ellie, lass," said Pa in his rich warm voice. "I don't want to hear any more of your bad-talkin' the teacher. You've been brought up to show respect!"

"Keep a civil tongue in your head," said Mother, crossly.

And that was that. Maggie held her tongue and left for school.

This morning, for the first time, she was riding Belle to school since Pa would be stooking all day and wouldn't need the team. "So," Mother had said, "you might as well ride the mare instead of using shank's mare."

Maggie had to climb up on the well casing in the barnyard to get onto Belle's broad back. She clutched the reins in one hand, Belle's mane in the other, and jumped. Thump! She was lying across Belle on her stomach, her head down. She had to scramble to a sitting position, her long skirt getting in the way. Finally she was seated, her full skirt modestly covering her knees. Belle looked around a few times during this performance, but stood patiently until Maggie said, "Git up," exactly as she had heard Pa say it to the team.

It was a slow ride. The horse was tired from her long days in the wheat fields, and she ambled along, stopping to drink at a puddle, shaking her head and sniffing the breeze before she resumed her plodding.

When they finally got to school, Maggie put Belle in the shed with the other horses and ponies. There were five animals, each in its own narrow stall, and a large space at the back which held some fresh straw and a few old horse blankets. She slipped the mare's bridle off and hung it on a nail. Belle's leather halter was under the bridle, with the rope looped around her neck. Maggie tied the halter rope to the manger. She took a minute to rub the white strip between Belle's eyes and murmur to the big, quiet beast. Belle's calm, intelligent eyes looked into hers. A fly lighted on Belle's withers, and her skin quivered until the fly flew away to join the others buzzing around the horses in the other stalls.

Maggie was late. When she went into the schoolroom, she knew at once that something was up. She could feel an air of excitement. Then she saw the new boy. He was younger than Bert and Asa, but bigger than the little boys, so the teacher had put him in the middle of the row. He was strangely dressed, in a tweed wool suit with short pants. That must be itchy, she thought. It looked so hot and formal. In contrast to the other boys, who were all barefoot, he wore black, ankle-high boots and knee-high socks.

After lunch, Miss Prentiss was correcting some papers, a bored look on her face. Asa Ebenezer and Bert Philips were whispering loudly, but she paid no attention. Asa rose from his desk and stealthily crept along the aisle until he came to an empty desk behind the new boy. He squeezed into the seat and looked back at Bert, who was shaking with silent laughter. Then Asa took the cork out of an ink bottle and held it above the boy's head. The boy was busy writing out spelling words on his slate and didn't know Asa was behind him. Maggie was afraid of what Asa might do. She waved her arm in the air, trying to get the teacher's attention. She knew she mustn't speak out, because, although Miss Prentiss allowed all sorts of goings-on in class, she refused to answer any student who spoke to her directly.

Slowly and deliberately, Asa tipped the ink bottle. A thin stream of black ink hit the boy's collar and dripped down the back of his suit jacket. Bert couldn't contain himself any longer. He whooped with laughter. Miss Prentiss finally looked up.

"Asa!" she shouted. "What are you doing? Get back to your seat!"

Asa looked back at Bert, who was still laughing. This seemed to give him courage.

"What are you doing?" the teacher repeated.

"Just helping the English boy," Asa answered. Then he got bolder. "I thought I'd learn him to talk proper. Nobody can make out what he's goin' on about." He looked again over his shoulder. All the big boys were laughing now, and Asa smiled. Never before had anyone spoken so boldly to the teacher. He drew himself up in his seat as if proud of himself, but he was watching Miss Prentiss for her reaction.

The new boy turned in his seat. His cheeks were burning red in his pale face. Maggie didn't care what Miss Prentiss did or said; she got out of her seat and handed the boy her handkerchief. "There's ink on the back of your neck," she said.

"Ellie. Sit down this minute or I shall tell your father how disrespectful you are!"

Maggie sat down. She had never been so angry with a teacher! Miss Prentiss was shouting at her instead of at Asa. Then a thought crossed her mind — perhaps Miss Prentiss was afraid of Asa.

Maybe Asa had the same thought, because he looked quite cocky. "I think it's recess time, Miss," he said. And he got up and walked from the room. When he got to the door, he turned and waited. First Bert, then the other big boys, stood and followed Asa outside. The younger boys looked scared, but they did what Asa wanted and trotted along behind the big boys.

Miss Prentiss' eyes grew big and round. Her mouth opened and closed a few times before she found her voice. Then she said to the four girls and the new boy, the only students still in the room, "One word out of any of you and I'm getting out the strap!"

There was silence in the room, except for little Mary's sniffles. Miss Prentiss strode back and forth across the front of the room, her face angry and forbidding. Maggie slumped down in her seat, full of misery. She wished she could tell Pa and Mother what was going on at school, but she had learned one thing about school in the 1800s — no child was allowed to criticize a teacher.

At supper that night, Pa chattered on about all the news he had picked up in the nearby town, Valhalla, where he'd gone that afternoon to fetch supplies. Maggie was only half-listening, her mind still on school, when suddenly she heard every word Pa said, clear as a bell.

"Yep. Home Children, they call 'em. Poor little mites bein' sent out from the Old Country to work on farms. Orphans, most of 'em. Newt Ebenezer got one off the train yesterday. Says he needs the help, since he has only one boy in the family. Yep, some English boy's goin' to have a hard life, seein' as he's goin' to the Ebenezers'. It don't seem fair." And Pa shook his head at the wicked ways of the world.

No, it isn't fair, thought Maggie. It's not fair that anybody should have to give up their real home and be forced to live here in this horrible place!

Chapter Seven

The Home Boy

From the time that Nicholas got off the train in Valhalla and met the man who was to be his master for the next three years, he had been afraid.

The other passengers on the train from Winnipeg had stared at him in his tight wool jacket and short wool pants. There was a label pinned to his lapel, as if he were a parcel. The label said: "NICHOLAS CAMPER to be delivered to MR. NEWTON EBENEZER, VALHALLA, MANITOBA."

He went into the station and sat on a bench, but no one spoke to him. Finally everyone was gone but him and the station agent. He was afraid to ask questions, so he sat alone on the bench, wondering if anyone would come. If no one did, would they send him back on the next train?

Miss Charity, the lady who ran the orphanage in London, England, where he had been living for the last few months, had sent him here. He didn't know if that was really her name or if people called her that because of her work with the young beggars and pickpockets who roamed the streets of London because their parents were either impoverished or dead.

The orphanage was run with military precision. The boys slept in rows of iron cots on the third floor. After evening prayers, they washed and went to bed. After 8:30, any boy who was caught speaking, even one word, would be punished.

The rougher boys hated life at the orphanage, for most of them had been living by their wits on the streets and weren't used to all the rules. But Nicholas didn't mind the place because it provided clean clothes and decent food.

He hadn't had much of either since his father had been killed. When he was small, he had lived with his parents in clean little rooms over his father's shop. When he was only four years old, he had learned to read the sign over the shop door: *Nicholas Camper — Master Bootmaker*. He was so proud when he read that sign. He knew even then that his father had an excellent reputation and there was great demand for his well-fitted boots made of the finest leathers.

Nicholas remembered the day the bailiffs came, a few weeks after his father died. They said his father had borrowed money, and now that he was dead his mother must pay. At first she hadn't believed them and told them to leave. Then they showed her some crumpled papers bearing his father's signature, and the spirit went out of her. Within a few weeks she sold everything, paid the debts and went out looking for work as a seamstress. Their home became one room.

Nicholas was sure that it was the damp and mould in their dingy room that caused her cough. As she got sicker and weaker, she sewed less and less. She did a bit of needlework for the Lost Lambs Orphanage, but made so little he had to resort to begging for food. That's when Miss Charity had convinced his mother he'd be better off living in the orphanage.

Every few months, Miss Charity brought a group of her boys to Canada and found places for them on farms and in fishing villages, where they would live and work. She promised that all the boys would be given good food and clothing, and a decent home. They would go to school on weekdays and to church on Sundays. They would be paid a few dollars each month for their work (he couldn't remember how much because Canadian money meant nothing to him). She also said that a Home Inspector would make sure these arrangements were kept.

The days and nights blurred together on the long voyage from London to Montreal. There were fifty children from the orphanage travelling out to Canada on the ship, and at least half of them were seasick.

Nicholas lay on his berth, his eyes closed, feeling the pitch of the ship, his teeth clenched against the urge to throw up when there was nothing left in his stomach.

Miss Charity was not sick for a moment on the rolling ship. In fact, she seemed to be invigorated by the sea air. He remembered her lining up all fifty of her charges on the deck for morning prayers and lecturing them on their weakness. They shouldn't allow themselves to give in to sickness, she said. They had a duty to the British Empire and to the Lost Lambs Orphanage to be strong workers for the good families who would be taking them in and treating them as their own. Canada was a new country with unlimited opportunities. They should all be grateful for this wonderful chance to better themselves.

In Montreal, Miss Charity put the children going west on the train with their new addresses pinned to their suit jackets. From then on they were on their own. Nicholas could still feel the slow rocking of the CPR car, with its hard benches, day after day on its long journey to Winnipeg. He had stretched out on the dirty floor beside his bench to get a little sleep at night. Someone had stepped on his leg, and he still had an ugly bruise.

"Nicholas Camper?" His name was shouted at him, as if he was deaf. A tall, stooped man stood in the doorway of the station. He wore an old felt hat pulled low on his forehead, and beneath the brim were pale empty eyes. He wore dirty clothes, and his elbows stuck out through holes in his sleeves. He had a big wad of something in his cheek and, when the man spoke, Nicholas could see his teeth were stained brown.

"Jus' look," the man said to the station agent. "I need a good strong lad, and they send me a skinny runt."

Nicholas' heart sank. He had been imagining his new home ever since he had boarded the ship in London. Never once had he imagined being greeted with such coldness.

They left the station, and the man swung Nicholas' little metal trunk onto the back of the wagon. He climbed onto the seat beside him, shouted at the team of old brown horses, and they began their journey to Nicholas' new home.

On the long journey, neither spoke. Nicholas stared in amazement at the same landscape he had seen from the windows of the train: mile after mile of prairie grasses, the vista broken intermittently with a few fields of grain or some poor little buildings. He had lived all his life in London, with buildings crowding against one another, cobblestone streets filled with jostling, horse-drawn cabs and drays. And people, everywhere, talking and laughing and crying and fighting. If someone had told him there was a part of the world as empty and quiet as this, he would not have believed it.

The man chewed the wad and spit long streams of tobacco juice over the side of the wagon. Nicholas sank down in fear, misery and loneliness.

His new home was a log building with a sod roof and a dirt floor. The man led him inside, climbed a ladder and opened a trapdoor in the ceiling. He hauled the little trunk upstairs, and Nicholas followed. The man left him, and Nicholas knew this must be where he would sleep. There was no window, but there were chinks between the logs that let some light in. In the dimness, Nicholas could make out a sagging cot against the wall, with a dirty mattress and one rough blanket.

He stayed there, sitting on the edge of the bed, until he heard his name shouted from below. He could smell the rich scent of meat frying. His stomach ached and he realized how hungry he was. He hadn't eaten since the train left Winnipeg that morning. He scampered down the stairs. A little woman, thin except for a bulging stomach, wearing a threadbare grey dress, was putting a platter of pork chops on the table beside a big bowl of steaming boiled potatoes.

"Here, boy," she said, motioning to a chair at one side of a long table.

He sat beside two little girls. Across the table sat a bigger girl they called Cora, and a strong-looking, stocky boy they called Asa. The mother helped the little girls by cutting their meat. Cora didn't say anything, but he could see her studying him from under her lashes as she ate. There was no plate in front of Nicholas, so he waited patiently, licking his lips as the smells of the hot food surrounded him.

Newt Ebenezer filled his plate. Asa grabbed the platter from his father and took a thick chop, dripping with brown juices. He plunked the meat down on top of a mound of potatoes, cut the meat into large pieces, dropped his knife and began forking huge mouthfuls of potatoes and meat into his mouth. Nicholas watched in amazement as Asa swallowed without chewing.

Newt Ebenezer was busily gobbling his mound of potatoes and meat. He scooped up a large slice of homemade bread, held it in one hand, spread it thickly with butter and stuffed half of it in his mouth in one motion.

The woman served the girls some potatoes, then she went to the stove. She came back to the table with a plate which she put in front of Nicholas. He looked down into a watery pool of beans and molasses. He looked up into the woman's face, confused. Her eyes were downcast, as if she were ashamed. She scurried to her seat and helped herself to the last pork chop on the platter.

"What's this, boy? Did you think you would get the same food as your betters?" growled Newt.

Nicholas quickly began eating the beans, afraid someone might snatch them away before he could finish them. When he reached, tentatively, for a slice of bread, no one seemed to notice. But when his fingers touched the butter dish, Newt grabbed it out of his hand with no comment and passed it to Asa. The boy looked at Nicholas as he spread butter on his second helping of potatoes. Then he glanced at his father as if seeking approval.

After supper, Nicholas was sent to the attic. It seemed he had just dropped into an exhausted sleep when he was shaken awake. The woman was standing at the side of his bed in the dimness.

"It's five in the morning, boy. Time for work. You got work clothes in there?" She pointed at his trunk.

He nodded. When she left, he quickly dressed in the heavy cotton shirt and long work pants provided by the orphanage. He wore the thin socks and ill-fitting boots he had arrived in.

There was a bowl of porridge for Nicholas, while Asa and Newt ate fried eggs, ham, bread and coffee. Then Newt told Nicholas to "git to that barn, or I'll know the reason why."

In the barn, the rank smell of manure hit him like a physical blow. Clouds of flies buzzed and hovered over the filthy floor and the poor animals with manure matted to their hides. Newt yelled at Nicholas to start milking. The frightened boy from the streets of London had never seen a live cow before. He had no idea how to go about milking one. Asa was milking in the next stall. Nicholas stared at how he was doing it until Newt handed him a stool and a bucket. Newt left him there and busied himself feeding the horses.

Nicholas sat at a cow, as he saw Asa sit, and began pulling on the cow's udder, but nothing came out. He pulled harder. Still nothing. Newt was walking toward him. Nicholas saw the black scowl on his face, and he felt panic rising in his throat. This time he pulled harder, squeezing at the same time. Perhaps he pinched, because the cow kicked. He didn't see it coming, but suddenly he felt a heavy blow and he was lying in a pile of manure behind the cow. He lay still for a moment, sure his leg was broken. In a moment, he was able to struggle to his feet. Asa was uttering a loud, nervous laugh.

"I won't whip you this time," shouted Newt. "The cow's smarter than you are. She gave you your whippin' for today."

Newt handed Nicholas a pitchfork and told him to start cleaning the barn. Nicholas struggled to carry forkfuls of manure and straw to a huge pile outside the door. After Newt and Asa finished the milking, the woman came to collect the pails of milk. She looked at Nicholas with an impassive face, but Nicholas imagined there was a flicker of pity in her eyes.

Nicholas was then ordered to water the cattle at the creek. "If I find one of these cows gets in a field of grain for even one mouthful, I'll whip ya 'til ya can't stand," threatened Newt.

Nicholas did the best he could. He didn't know anything about cattle, but the cows knew the way to the water and he found all he had to do was follow them. It was getting them back to the barn for the night that was a challenge. Fed, watered and milked, there was nothing to entice them back the way they had come. They wanted to graze. They kept stopping, and when Nicholas ran up behind two or three, yelling at them to keep going, others took advantage of his absence to wander over to a greener patch of grass. After nearly an hour of running and shouting, he finally got the cows back to the barn.

"Where was you, boy? You're late!" shouted Newt Ebenezer. Nicholas trembled.

"Sorry, sir," he mumbled, afraid to speak out because he was learning that his accent would set the man off on a tirade.

And so began life for Nicholas with the Ebenezers. Never enough sleep, never enough food, long days of exhausting work, much of it strange and incomprehensible to the city boy. He learned to run when he was called, and never to let up at a task, even if he felt his back would break. In this way he avoided beatings, but whenever he said or did something that Newt Ebenezer disapproved of, he got a sharp cuff on the ear. Matilda Ebenezer seemed to pity him, but she never had a kind word for him. Nicholas felt that was because she, too, was afraid of her husband. Sometimes she put a little cold meat and butter on his bread in the lunch pail he took with him while he herded the cows. Cora never smiled at him or spoke when others were around, but once, when Newt was away, she came to the barn and gave Nicholas a lesson on milking cows. These small kindnesses gave him courage.

His new life was not what Nicholas had been promised. This grim little farm was nothing like the big estates with immense fields of golden wheat that he had seen pictures of in the orphanage. Miss Charity had told him that he was bound to work on the farm until he was sixteen. He wouldn't be sixteen for three years! How would he bear this misery for three whole years?

Knowing about the Home Inspector gave Nicholas hope. He was certain that as soon as an inspector saw how he was being treated, he would be moved to a better place. All he had to do was hold out until the inspector arrived.

When Matilda Ebenezer told him one morning to change into his suit after milking because he'd be going to school today, he was very excited. He had been to school in England only for the few months he had lived in the orphanage. He longed to read well enough to master whole books.

But his tormentor, Asa, went to school with him. Nicholas soon saw that the other boys at school followed Asa's example, and they all made fun of his accent and his clothes. The teacher didn't pay much attention to him, and he was afraid he would never learn much.

The hardest thing to bear in this new country was the fact that he was thousands of miles away from his mother, whom he missed dreadfully. Night after night, Nicholas crept silently upstairs to his attic, tired, aching and heartsick. But he was never too tired to reach into his trunk, under his few pieces of cheap clothing, to pull out the cracked, curling photo of his mother, taken before his father died.

His mother had come to say goodbye just before he boarded the ship to Canada. That day, she had brushed his hair back from his forehead and peered into his eyes. He was thirteen, she said, almost grown up. And he was just like his father. She was wrong, he knew. His father hadn't been afraid of anything. Not even the runaway horses that had killed him in the street.

When Nicholas said goodbye to his mother, he held her thin hands and made a pledge that he would make a home for both of them in Canada. "Just wait for me, Mum," he had said. "I'll send for you."

Now he curled up on his hard cot and pulled the blanket over his head so no one would hear him crying — heartbroken because he was certain he would never be able to keep his promise to bring his mother to Canada.

Chapter Eight

Barn Fire!

Asa and Cora drove the three miles from their home to school, and Nicholas walked. The teacher listened to him read, then she put him in the fourth book with the younger boys. When he stumbled over the words, all the boys sniggered at his English accent. At recess, they chased him around the school, calling, "Limey! Limey!" Miss Prentiss pretended she didn't notice what was going on.

At noon hour, Nicholas finished his meagre lunch inside the schoolroom with the girls. Then he went to stand in the shade of the school, where he looked longingly across the yard toward the barn. He was trying to get enough courage to join the other boys. Maybe if he swaggered in, as if he were afraid of nothing, they would have more respect for him. Just thinking of it made his throat tighten and his mouth go dry, but he didn't know what else to do. He couldn't stand being shut out forever.

As he was trying to get the courage to move, he saw the girl, Ellie, walking toward the barn. She was the only one who had been openly kind to him since he had come to this big, empty country. But he didn't dare talk to her because he knew the other boys would tease him. She must be going to the barn to feed the hairy-footed horse she rode to school.

Nicholas had had a terrible fear of horses ever since the police had come to the little flat over his father's bootmaking shop with the news that his father had been killed by a runaway team of horses. Nicholas hadn't seen those horses, but he had a picture of them in his mind that was so clear, sometimes he couldn't believe he hadn't actually seen the accident. He dreamed of that scene, night after night. In his dream, two huge black horses were rearing above his father, who was lying in the street. Their giant hooves were pawing the air above his head, their eyes rolling, and ribbons of smoke and fire shooting from their nostrils.

Ellie's horse was big and black. He hated and feared that horse as much as he did the bullies in the barn. And because he was so frightened, he despised himself.

That slight girl, Ellie, seemed to be afraid of nothing. She strode into the barn as if she had a right to be there. In a minute or two, she came back. She stopped when she saw him and smiled. Then she looked puzzled as he clenched his fists and, without speaking, walked past her toward the barn. His breath was coming in shallow gasps. The palms of his hands were wet with sweat.

As he neared the barn door, it was slammed in his face. He could hear a high reedy voice saying, "Me nime is Nicholas Camper and Oim a Limey from Lon'n." This was followed by gales of laughter. It was Asa mocking him. Nicholas turned, his head bowed, and walked slowly back toward the school.

When Miss Prentiss rang the bell for class, none of the boys came out of the barn.

The classroom was quiet and orderly without Asa and Bert to stir up trouble. Miss Prentiss seemed agitated. She kept glancing at the door as if she expected the boys to come back at any moment. Mary and Rosie recited their lessons. The teacher leapt to her feet when the doorknob rattled, but it was only Billy Cranbrook, one of the younger boys who was in the fourth book with Nicholas. He had straw stuck to the legs of his pants, and his eyes were wide and frightened.

"Please, Miss," he shouted. "The barn's on fire. And we can't get the horses out. They's too scared to move!"

Before the teacher could respond, Ellie was out of her seat. She streaked past the teacher and out the door. "Belle," she shouted over her shoulder. "I've got to get my horse out!"

Nicholas didn't stop to think. He leapt to his feet and ran after Ellie. The other boys were milling about outside the barn. Smoke was puffing out the doorway. A horse whinnied, loud and frightened. Nicholas saw Ellie run past the boys, cover her mouth and nose with her sleeve, and plunge into the barn. He had been running at her heels, but he stopped at the open door.

He could see smoke coming out of the straw at the back of the barn. Ellie's horse was stamping and pulling at its rope, its eyes white and rolling. Ellie sidled along the edge of the stall to the horse's head, undid the rope and tried to back Belle out of the stall. But Belle quivered, shook her head up and down, and neighed as the smoking straw burst into flame.

Nicholas knew he should help Ellie. He wanted to help her. Suddenly Belle backed out of the stall, pulling the rope from Ellie's hand. The effect was so sudden that Ellie fell backward as the big mare dashed toward the door. Nicholas just had time to throw himself to the ground out of her way. From the ground he could feel as much as see the big black animal thundering past.

By the time Ellie staggered outside, Belle was galloping down the trail toward home. As Nicholas got to his feet, Bert and Asa brushed past him with buckets of water. They threw the water over the burning pile of straw. Soon the fire was out, and the horses and ponies were all outside, safe. Bert and Asa strutted around, acting proud and boastful about saving the horses.

Miss Prentiss was beside herself, shouting at the boys.

"How did this happen?"

"Please, Miss," said Billy.

"Shut up," said Asa, menacingly.

But Billy was frightened. His smoke-blackened face was streaked with tears. For once, he wasn't going to listen to Asa.

"We was having a smoke," he sobbed. "Every day we smokes in the barn. We didn't mean to start a fire. It was just an accident."

· · ·

While walking home, Maggie met Pa, coming to get her.

"What happened, lass?" he asked, worry showing on his round face. She couldn't answer until he told her that Belle was safe, at home in her stall. Then she told Pa all about the boys staying out of school and of how they set fire to the barn. When she told about untying Belle and trying to get her out of the barn, he stopped in his tracks, speechless.

"That Asa is just a big bully!" she said angrily. "I feel really sorry for poor Nicholas, having to live with him. And just think!" she went on, the words pouring out the frustration and fear, "Belle might have burned to death!"

For once, Pa didn't scold her for her criticizing. He didn't even scold her for going into a burning barn. That would come later. Now, his mouth was set in a straight line and his eyes were serious.

"I'll tell you, Ellie, lass," he said putting his big hand gently on her shoulder. "I had no idea there was such goin's-on at school. We can't have that — not at all, not at all. And I guess it's up to the school board to do somethin' about it!"

Chapter Nine

Penny and Copper

When Pa came home from the school board emergency meeting, he looked at Mother, his eyes dancing, then he turned to Maggie and said, "I have news for you, lassie. Miss Prentiss has had to resign as teacher. It seems she's needed to help her parents on their farm. We've written to Winnipeg and asked for a strong man teacher to manage those bullies!"

Maggie felt like shouting, but knew she'd better not. She clasped her hands in front of her and rose up and down on her toes. She was trying to keep from dancing, which would mean a lecture from Mother. A strong man teacher would get control of the school so people could learn. She just hoped that the man would be a good teacher as well as being strong.

"I have more news!" Pa said. Maggie's heels came down on the floor. Whatever was he talking about?

Pa was looking at Mother now, as he talked. "Miss Prentiss has been living at home, as you know. The new teacher will have to board with somebody in the district. I told them that we had the room here."

"What? You told them what?" Mother sputtered. "Three little rooms is all we've got. Where will we put the teacher to sleep? Hang him on a nail in the corner?"

"Now, now, Mother!" said Pa. "We could use some cash money, and a teacher pays eight dollars per month room and board. Since we raise most of our food, that money's clear profit."

Mother still looked angry, but she stopped arguing. That night at the supper table, Maggie found out why.

"I've been thinking, Pa," Mother said. "We can make do with the teacher here for a few months by putting Ellie out in the lean-to. The teacher can have her room."

Maggie's head snapped up. She hadn't been consulted about giving up her room, and she didn't look forward to squeezing her bed and clothes-box into the little shed attached to the end of the house. It was already crammed with buckets, a wash boiler, two washtubs, a scrub board, Mother's gardening tools, and an old cupboard full of jams and pickles. Maggie was starting to wonder if this new teacher was going to be just a lot of trouble.

"Fine, fine," said Pa, nodding his head, thinking he'd won the argument.

"I was wondering how the new teacher will get to school every day?" Mother asked casually.

"Walk. I suppose he'll walk with Ellie, here," Pa said, as if his mind were on something else.

"Oh, that would never do," said Mother firmly. "If we are going to board the teacher, we've got to supply him with decent transportation."

"Well, I suppose he and Ellie could ride Belle and Bess when I don't need the team for farmin'."

"And how often would that be? You use them 'most every day for something. No, Pa. If we're going to board the teacher, we have to get a decent team of drivers so the teacher and Ellie can go to school in the buggy."

Pa looked startled. "A team of drivers! Now where would we get that kind of money?"

Mother didn't say a word, but opened the cupboard door and took down a crock from the top shelf. She pulled out a wad of bills and began counting.

"That's to buy more milk cows," sputtered Pa. "We've got to build up our herd if we're ever goin' to get ahead in this farmin' game! And besides!" — his voice sounded triumphant, as if he'd just thought of the winning argument — "we have to build up the farm if we're ever goin' to build that new house you're always talkin' about."

"It was your decision to board the teacher," Mother responded in a voice that showed she had made up her mind and nothing would change it. "Now it's my turn to have a say. I'm saying that we need a decent team of drivers. We've got a good crop coming, and as soon as we sell the grain we'll have enough for a few more cows. We'll build up our farm and we'll get the new house one of these days. I don't want the neighbours thinking we're poorer than we are. We need a decent team."

"I thought somebody told me we shouldn't count our chickens before they're hatched," said Pa. "The crop isn't threshed yet."

"Oh ye of little faith," said Mother. She had made a decision, and that was that.

A few days later, Pa hitched Bess and Belle to the light wagon and drove off. When he came into the yard late that afternoon, Bess and Belle were tied to the back of the wagon, and Pa was driving a beautiful pair of matched horses with long black manes and tails. Their chestnut coats shone in the slanting rays of the setting sun. Maggie ran to watch them come up the lane. The new horses were fine-boned and elegant. When they trotted, it was if they were dancing on their long graceful legs, necks arched and their feet lifted high. Pa looked proud. Mother came out the door and stood on the doorstep. Pa pulled up in front of her and stepped to the ground. He put an arm across his middle and made a bow.

"Would you care to go for a drive, m'lady?"

Mother hitched up her skirts, and Pa helped her climb up to the high seat of the wagon. Mother took the reins, clicked her tongue and drove off toward the barn. She drove with her back ramrod stiff, her chin up, her voice quiet but strong, letting the horses know she was in command.

Maggie and Pa stood on the step, watching Mother drive those beautiful horses. "That's what I noticed first about your mother when I was courtin' her," said Pa, his voice full of admiration. "What a stylish driver she is."

Maggie could tell that his eyes were full of Mother. But her eyes were full of nothing but those pretty chestnut horses shining in the sun. Her heart was beating hard. This must be what it feels like when you fall in love, she thought.

• • •

School was closed until the new teacher arrived. Nobody was worried about this interruption because it was threshing time and many of the children were needed to help, so they wouldn't have been at school anyway.

Mother and Ellie had to get ready for the threshers, who were moving through the district, from farm to farm, with their huge machine, separating the grain from the straw. They were at the south end of the district now. It was hard to judge just how long they'd be, Pa said, but they would come soon.

Mother began preparations for their arrival by making some pound cakes and storing them in crocks. Then she and

Maggie made green tomato-pickles and stored them in more crocks in the back kitchen. Next, Maggie spent hours chopping cabbages for Mother to put up sauerkraut. Maggie was thoroughly sick of this boring task, when Pa said he needed Ellie to help him. Mother, probably thinking of the new drivers, let him have his way.

Maggie was ecstatic. She loved working in the barn with the animals. Behind the barn was a corral where the new horses were kept. She stood outside the poplar-rail fence, drinking in their beauty.

"Brother and sister, Ellie," said Pa leaning on the fence post beside her. "That's why they're such a good match. A filly and a gelding. Two and three years old."

Maggie thought the filly, with a white star on her face, was the prettier one. But the gelding, whose four white feet flashed a pretty pattern when he trotted, was handsome as well.

"What are their names, Pa?" she asked.

"Now that's what I wanted to talk to you about. The man I bought them from called them Flossie and Herb. He named them after his in-laws. Now, I don't think those are any kinda' names for pretty horses like these. I figure they're ours now, so it's up to us to give them names that fit better, somehow. Got any ideas, lass?"

Maggie joined in laughing with Pa at the idea of calling these beautiful horses Flossie and Herb. She thought hard for a few moments. The filly nipped the gelding on the shoulder and they both tossed their heads, the light glinting off them.

"Pa," she began hesitantly, "their coats shine in the sun like new coins. How about calling them Penny and Copper?"

"Penny and Copper," Pa repeated slowly. "Penny and Copper." Then a slow smile spread across his face. "I think you've just discovered their names, Ellie. I could swear that filly just nodded her head as if you guessed right. As if those were their names all along, but they couldn't tell anybody."

Pa let Maggie brush Penny and Copper while they were tied safely to a fence post. He warned her that they were young and skittish, not placid and slow like Bess and Belle. She had to be extra careful, and not fool around with them unless he was with her. He said that Mother would skin him alive if she got hurt by one of them.

"You're too young to manage them, lassie, but when we get the new teacher he'll be able to watch out for you. Then I'll let you drive them to school on the days that Mother isn't usin' them."

"What about riding them?" asked Maggie. She took a deep breath and stated something she only guessed might be true. "You know I'm good at riding, Pa. Maybe I could ride one to bring in the cows."

"It's true you're a fine little rider, but, as I say, these two are young and skittish. And your mother wouldn't approve, if she knew." Pa shook his head, looking from Maggie to the horses. Maggie knew he was wavering.

Maggie took another chance and said, "Remember how many times I fell off when I was learning to ride? Falling off one of these horses wouldn't be any different from that."

But Pa didn't want to go too far too fast. "I don't know what they're like, yet, lass. Horses are like people, you know. Some are smart, some aren't. Some are foolish, some are wise. Just take it slow, and get to know these youngsters and let them get to know you, then we'll see."

Maggie took him at his word, and every time she had a free moment she was with the new horses. When she was hanging clothes on the line, she would run to the barn between loads and rub Penny's and Copper's noses. When she was scrubbing the worn boards of the kitchen floor on Saturday morning, she rushed so she would have a few minutes with the horses before it was time to set the bread for afternoon baking. While the bread was browning in the oven, she ran to the barn with a few carrots from the garden to feed her horses.

By now, Maggie thought of Penny and Copper as *her* horses. She didn't mind Mother driving them into town when she needed tea, sugar or salt on Saturday afternoon. Or Mother driving them to a neighbour's farm for a Ladies' Aid meeting. Because, when Mother got home, tired from her outing, she turned the horses over to her enthusiastic daughter. Then Maggie rubbed them down, fed and watered them and talked to them.

Before long, when Penny and Copper heard Maggie's voice, or saw her running toward the barnyard, long hair swinging, they would whicker and trot to the fence and wait for her.

One day, Pa came out of the barn just as Penny lipped a piece of turnip from Maggie's hand. Copper stamped and snorted, reminding her that he was waiting for his treat.

"I think today's the day, lassie," Pa said. Maggie knew immediately what he was talking about.

Maggie bridled Penny, then Pa held the filly's head with one hand and he cupped his other hand so Maggie could step into it and be hoisted onto Penny's bare back. He opened the gate of the corral with the words, "Careful now. Take it slow."

As soon as Penny was out the gate, she started to prance on her dainty hooves. She felt the light weight of the girl on her back and the freedom of being outside the fence. Maggie held the reins tightly, murmuring in a calm voice, but Penny couldn't be contained. She shook her head wildly and took off into the wind.

The girl and the filly streaked across the prairie. At home in the twentieth century, Maggie always rode with a saddle. Now, riding bareback for the first time, she felt her body slipping first one way, then the other. Instinctively, she gripped the horse with her knees, pulled on the reins with one hand and grasped Penny's mane with the other. The air was rushing past her ears, so she couldn't hear, but, in moments, she sensed something entering her line of vision from the left. It was another moment before she realized that it was Copper. Copper was galloping alongside Penny.

Maggie was afraid that, with Copper alongside, Penny would keep running as long as he did, and that might be for hours. She let go of the coarse black mane and grasped the reins hard in both hands. She felt herself slipping, but there was nothing she could do to stop.

The sudden thud as her body hit the ground jarred through her. It was like there was an explosion in her head. She lay perfectly still, trying to breathe, trying to clear her vision. She felt the terrible taste of defeat. She hadn't been able to manage Penny, just like Pa had warned.

She squeezed her eyes shut, holding back the stinging hot tears. Then, she felt something warm and soft on her cheek, like a kiss. She opened her eyes to see Penny's muzzle only inches away.

She sat up, amazed. Penny had stopped! This skittish filly, who, only moments before she had been thinking was too wild for her, had stopped in her headlong rush to freedom on the prairie. She had stopped because Maggie had fallen!

Maggie sat up, carefully testing her arms and legs for breaks. When she was satisfied that she was only bruised, she got painfully to her feet. It was then she saw Copper. He was grazing only a few metres away.

Maggie led Penny to a little bluff of trees. It took perhaps ten or fifteen minutes of trying and failing, but finally she was able to get Penny positioned properly, then use a stump as a step to climb onto her back.

The ride home was brisk, with both horses still full of energy, but this time Maggie was in control, and when they came in sight of the barnyard and met Pa riding Belle coming to fetch them, she was able to pull Penny to a stop. Copper followed suit.

"Are you all right, lass?" were Pa's first words. He didn't wait for her to answer because he could see that she was. He pulled Belle up beside her.

"I've never seen anything like it in my life! That little filly takes off like a bat outa Hades, and then the colt sails over the fence, slick as can be. By the time I got Belle bridled up and outa the barn, you was nowheres to be seen." He shook his head.

When Maggie told him what had happened, and how both horses had waited for her after she fell, he shook his head again.

"Remarkable. That's the only word for it. Remarkable! Now, when we get back to the barn, I want to try a little experiment."

Back in the corral, Pa bridled Copper and helped Maggie mount. This time, Maggie held him to a trot, but, within moments, there was Penny at their side. When she came back, Pa was laughing.

"Never saw nor heard of the likes of it. They can both jump a fence slick as a whistle, but they've been locked up together in here for days and never jumped it once. They don't want to be separated! That's the long and short of it. It looks to me that, when you're ridin' one, you're going to have the other followin' along, wherever you go!"

Maggie began rubbing down Penny with an old sack. Pa was rubbing down Copper. "And another thing we learned, today," Pa went on. "They've both got a lot of sense. When you slipped off, they didn't leave you. They're full of beans, but they can be trusted. That don't always happen."

Maggie smiled to herself. She was stiff and sore, but, in spite of that, she was happy. Pa was talking as if he expected her to go on riding her lovely horses. Living in Manitoba was turning out to be pretty exciting after all.

Chapter Ten

The New Teacher

When Pa picked up the mail at the post office in Valhalla, there was a letter addressed to him as chairman of the Victoria School Board. It was from the Department of Education in Winnipeg saying that a teacher by the name of C.R. Fieldmont would be arriving by train on Friday. Pa said that he would meet the new teacher at the station, since he would be boarding with them.

On Friday, Maggie volunteered to weed Mother's flower beds in front of the house so she could watch for Pa bringing the new man teacher home. She felt curious and excited and hopeful that all the problems at school would come to an end once the big boys saw a strong man at the front of the room.

She was scratching around the old-fashioned flowers, the mignonette and portulaca, when she spied Penny and Copper far down the trail. She smiled, as she always did, at the sight of her high-stepping drivers arching their graceful necks. The new teacher will be impressed, she thought. Then she could make out two figures in the buggy, one in dark clothes, one in light. There seemed to be a big bundle piled behind the figures. The next thing she noticed was that the passenger was a little shorter than Pa. This confused her, for most men were far taller than he was.

It wasn't until the buggy turned in to the lane that she was sure of what she was seeing, and ran inside to call Mother. Mother came out on the doorstep when Pa pulled up, said, "Whoa" to the horses, and got out to help the teacher step down. Mother and Maggie looked at each other, surprised. For, stepping out of the buggy, one slim arm extended for Pa to hold, was a petite young woman, dressed in an elegant hat and a light grey wrapper to keep the dust from her clothes.

"Mother, Ellie," said Pa formally, "This here's the new teacher, Miss Fieldmont." He was standing behind her, so he shrugged his shoulders to indicate he didn't understand how this could have happened.

Things got a little confusing then. Mother seemed uncharacteristically frazzled. For once, she didn't have anything to say. Maggie ran to help Pa, who was struggling to unload two large trunks and some leather cases tied to the back of the buggy.

The new teacher was pulling off her fine leather gloves, finger by finger. She surveyed the small whitewashed log house, its dusty front yard ornamented with little circles of flowers bordered with bleached buffalo bones. A washtub was hanging on a nail by the door, hens were scratching in the yard, and the sod-roofed barn was just down the path, with a big manure pile near the door. The barnyard was littered with crude log sheds, one for the chickens, one for the pigs, one for storing grain. Near the barn was an old sod building with yellow grasses growing on its roof. They all stood, waiting for her to speak, half afraid of what she would say.

"Just what I hoped to find," said Miss Fieldmont. "A real homestead in Manitoba, the land of opportunity! My, this will be an adventure!"

While Mother prepared tea and sandwiches, Miss Fieldmont told them her story. She was nineteen years old, and she had graduated that spring from a ladies' college in New Brunswick.

Just like me, thought Maggie. She came from New Brunswick to Manitoba just like me. But, of course, she couldn't say this to anyone.

It was at the college where Miss Fieldmont had seen a poster advertising teaching positions in the schools being built for people moving into the prairies to take up the free land called homesteads. She had been anxious to come, she said. Then she deftly turned the conversation away from herself with many questions about Victoria School.

That night, after Miss Fieldmont went to her room to rest, Pa looked at Mother and Mother looked at Pa.

"She can't last," said Mother. "Not in that school."

"We can't just ship her back, not all the way to New Brunswick," said Pa. "We'll have to wait and see how things sort themselves out." After he spoke, he uttered a deep sigh that seemed to come from the bottom of his boots.

Maggie felt a wave of disappointment begin in her chest and spread to her stomach. She thought the new teacher was fashionable and elegant, and at first she was excited about that. But she knew Pa and Mother were right. The big boys would make mincemeat out of her. Why, Bert and Asa and three or four of the other boys were bigger than she was.

The next day school reopened. It was a fine day, and Mother needed the buggy. She said she had to go to town to get a few things for the teacher's room. She apologized to the teacher for needing the horses. Miss Fieldmont said that was just fine, that actually she preferred to walk to school. She said it would be fine for her constitution. So she walked the two miles with Maggie.

Miss Fieldmont left the ruts to walk on the grass at the side of the trail to keep her neat kid boots, which just showed beneath her walking skirt, from getting dusty. Maggie strolled beside her. Big, fat clouds billowed around them in the prairie sky.

Maggie realized that her feet had toughened, and she could now walk almost anywhere without them hurting. So she plodded along, looking intently at the teacher to catch every expression.

She wanted to tell Miss Fieldmont about what had been going on in school, but she didn't know how.

"Ellie," said Miss Fieldmont, after a period of silence. "I understand you are the only older girl in the school. Why, when you think of it, " she added, "you're old enough to be my younger sister. I think we can speak freely with each other when we're together — like friends. But when we're at school, we must maintain proper decorum, and I'll be no more your friend than that of anyone else."

Maggie relaxed when she heard this. Then she told the teacher how Miss Prentiss had been run out by the big boys and how the boys had set the barn on fire.

They reached the school and Miss Fieldmont went in and looked around. She gingerly took the filthy towel off its nail on the back wall and dropped it on the floor. "We'll take turns bringing clean towels from home," she said. She peered into the full slop pail, where last week's hand-washing water had been dumped. "We'll take turns with all the chores," she said.

By nine o'clock, when the teacher rang the bell, the books in the library were sorted and the blackboard was washed. All the students but Nicholas had come to school today. They filed in quietly, sneaking shy little glances at the new teacher, taking her measure as they took their seats. Maggie was disappointed that Nicholas wasn't there.

Miss Fieldmont rose from where she sat at the unpainted table-desk, took a little pitch pipe from her pocket and blew a single note. Then, in a clear sweet voice, she began singing "The Ash Grove." From under the hem of her skirt, one tiny foot, booted in soft kid, beat the rhythm. The thin quavers of the girls and the little boys followed half a beat behind. The teacher glared at the big boys at the back of the room. They stood awkwardly, shifting their feet a little and looking at their hands, but they weren't singing.

Miss Fieldmont stopped singing, and the students' voices straggled to a halt. Miss Fieldmont tightened her grip on the shaved poplar stick she was using as a baton and said quietly, "Boys at the back, we are *all* to sing. It is part of our curriculum. If you refuse, I will be forced to take action."

She raised her pitch pipe slowly to her lips, glaring all the while at the big boys. They were taking furtive glances at each other. The little children in the front rows looked white and scared.

Before they could resume singing, there was a loud knock at the door. It was Mr. Trent, a young homesteader who was on the school board. He was dressed in a flannel shirt and trousers with wide suspenders. He was of medium height and his face was plain and craggy, but, when he smiled, his white teeth flashed attractively in his deeply tanned face. Maggie knew how busy the homesteaders were in the fields, but Mr. Trent, like the boys who had left the fields to come to school today, couldn't contain his curiosity.

"How is everyone settling in for the new teacher?" he asked, looking at the big boys in the back rows as he spoke.

Miss Fieldmont's eyes flashed. "I have everything under control, but thank you for asking," she said.

Mr. Trent looked surprised at the vehemence with which she spoke. He repeated two or three times that he had just come to say that, if she needed any help, the Board was with her all the way. Seeing that her manner was growing more distant and cold, he finally left, banging the door behind him. There were a few snickers from the back of the room, but Miss Fieldmont quickly quelled them with an icy look.

"It is time for arithmetic," she said. "We will continue with our music lesson Monday morning."

Maggie thought she detected the faintest of grins on the face of Asa Ebenezer. He looked as though he didn't mind waiting until Monday.

Chapter Eleven

Herding Cattle

$\mathcal{M}$aggie was happy when Saturday came because she would have more time to ride Penny and Copper. Pa liked the cattle to be able to graze on the prairie grasses far from the barn, but he couldn't let them wander on their own in case they got into the wheat fields which still hadn't been threshed. So Maggie could ride her horses and help Pa at the same time by keeping the cattle out of the grain.

"Don't cross the creek, Ellie," he warned her. "It's Newt Ebenezer's land on the other side. If any of the neighbours do anythin' to rile him, he gets mad as a bear with a sore paw."

Maggie took a book and some lunch that she tied in a cloth and hung over Penny's withers. The book was a collection of Greek and Roman myths she had found in the school library. Her plan was to have a ride on Penny, then a ride on Copper, then sit beneath a tree and read for a while, letting the horses graze alongside the cows.

She was lying under a tree, her chin in her hands, the book propped up in front of her, when Rambler stuck his cold black nose in her face. She laughed and pushed him away. He whined a little and ran away a short distance. She went on reading, but Rambler stuck his nose in her face again, whining and agitated. This time she sat up and looked around. Penny and Copper were grazing happily near her. Chub and Dora were drinking at the edge of the creek, which, at this time of year, had shrunk to a stream with a wide strip of dried black mud on either side. Blackie and Whitie had wandered downstream, but were still in view. Then she saw what was upsetting Rambler. Reddie and Blue were gone!

Quickly she mounted Penny, and rode the filly past Chub and Dora, across the creek and up the other bank, through the willows that bordered it. Copper trotted along by Penny's flank. On the other side of the willows, she reined in Penny and sat in amazement. There were strange cattle grazing on the lush prairie grass. Nine or ten of them. About a quarter-mile away there was a boy with a long willow switch running after some cows and yelling. It took Maggie only a moment to realize the cows he was trying to turn toward the creek were Reddie and Blue.

"Here, Rambler," Maggie called, and the shaggy little dog trotted up to Penny's side.

• • •

Nicholas was hot and tired. He didn't know who owned the two strange cows that had joined his herd, but he knew if Mr. Ebenezer saw them he would give him a beating. As soon as Nicholas got one cow turned back toward the creek in the direction from which it had come, the other doubled back to join the Ebenezers' cattle. He was running so hard and yelling so much, it took him by surprise when he looked past the cattle and saw a girl on a horse coming toward him. Another horse was trotting at their side, keeping pace as the girl's horse broke into a canter. It was the girl, Ellie, from school. He looked around, afraid that Mr. Ebenezer might be about, but when all he saw was the wide prairie and the cattle, he smiled a greeting.

Soon, with the help of her dog, Maggie and her horses had Reddie and Blue back on their own side of the creek. She left them there and rode back toward Nicholas.

All she said was, "Why didn't you come back to school?"

"Mr. Ebenezer needs me at home."

"Miss Fieldmont says it's the law that Home Children should attend school regularly. Is that true?"

"Yes, but he won't let me go. He says that I'm so lazy, he can't get enough work out of me. If I was in school the best part of the day, I wouldn't do enough to earn my keep."

Maggie snorted as if she was disgusted. She said that she had read about slaves and serfs, but she had never known one before. She said it was horrible and wrong, and someone should do something about it.

"No," said Nicholas sharply. He was thinking of what Mr. Ebenezer might do to him if the neighbours started meddling.

Maggie looked down at him from her horse, her forehead wrinkled. She seemed to be trying to figure something out. Then she asked if he'd like to do some schoolwork here, on the prairie. Nicholas didn't have to think about it. Of course he would like to! One thing that worried him about missing school was that he didn't read or write very well yet. He was afraid that this would hold him back from making his way in the world and bringing his mother to Canada.

So, they found a knoll that was high enough to give them a view of all the cattle, and they sat with Maggie's book between them, and he practised reading. It was a difficult book, but Maggie chimed in when the words were beyond him. Soon they were caught up in the story and didn't notice anymore who was reading what.

It was pleasant there on the prairie in the warmth of the afternoon. To the north, the faraway range of hills looked blue and hazy on the horizon. To the west, the stooks were standing in rows like soldiers, waiting for the threshers. To the east, the fields were almost bare, for Pa had hauled most of the sheaves closer to the farmstead, where they would be threshed. The long prairie grasses where the cattle grazed were yellow-dotted with goldenrod. Each little breeze lifted the leaves of the willow bushes along the creek, showing their white undersides.

Maggie read with him until it was almost time to go home for milking.

"Now," said Maggie, "before I go, would you like to have a ride on one of my horses?"

Nicholas felt something thump in his chest. It felt like there was a giant lump there, making it hard to breathe. The filly with the white star on her face was the one wearing the bridle. The gelding had only a halter, with the rope looped around his neck. He had never seen such beautiful, graceful creatures. One part of him longed to mount one of them and to gallop across the prairie, as if he didn't have a care in the world. But the knot of fear was there in his chest, growing every moment. Galloping hooves, shouting voices. A man lying dead in the street. Struck down and killed by unthinking, unreasoning power. A power that, once unleashed, no one could control.

"What's the matter?" asked the girl. "You've gone pale as a ghost."

He couldn't tell her why his hands were clenched. He couldn't tell anyone how terrified he was.

"I've never ridden before," was all he said.

"Oh, is that all!" said Maggie. "I remember learning to ride. It takes a bit of practice, that's all."

Then, without consulting him, she grasped the halter rope and led the gelding down to the creek, where he climbed on a clump of willows so he could jump onto Copper's back. When he hesitated, she told him not to worry, that she would lead the horse until he got used to sitting on it. He felt a little better then. Somehow the knowledge that she would keep control of the animal gave him the courage to scramble on. His fear returned after he was sitting very high, far above the ground. When the horse walked, the whole world became unstable. He hung on for dear life.

Maggie led the horse away from the creek and among the cows. Penny walked slowly after them for a moment, then went back to grazing, but with a wary eye on Copper in case he was taken away from her.

Nicholas felt the warmth of the shining chestnut coat. There was something strange about being so close to a living creature. With each step, his seat shifted a little. The moving shoulder blades rippled under the chestnut hide. He clung to the mane with both hands. The hair was strong and coarse.

"Pat his neck," said Maggie. "Talk to him. Let him get used to your voice."

Nicholas felt a little embarrassed. He bent down until he could smell the sweaty, dusty smell of Copper's coat. He rubbed his hand along the graceful neck. "Hello, Copper," he said.

The horse swung his head up and pricked up his ears. "Good boy," said Nicholas, lamely. Copper nodded his head twice, as if he understood. This animal was nothing like the horses in his dreams, the evil creatures that had taken away the life of his father. He started to relax a little.

Maggie led Copper to Penny, and quickly slipped off her bridle and put it on the gelding. Then she handed the reins to Nicholas and told him to ride a few minutes on his own, "just to get the feel of it."

Once again Nicholas felt the giant fist clutching his heart, but he grasped the reins. He had no choice! The girl was giving him instructions, but he hardly heard her. He became rigid as the horse began trotting. Suddenly he was bouncing, forgetting all about holding on with his legs, forgetting everything but his fear.

He wasn't thrown from the horse's back; he didn't fall off. In his rising panic, he threw himself from the monster. He thudded against the hard ground and lay there, his face hidden against his arms as he sprawled in the long grass. He heard the girl asking if he was hurt. He shook his head, but he was too ashamed to look up for a long time. When his breath finally slowed, he forced himself to sit up.

Maggie was sitting on the knoll, her horses grazing nearby. She was staring at him again, a puzzled look on her face.

He found the willow switch he had dropped, and began driving the cattle toward home. It was nearly milking time, so they went willingly. He heard the girl calling to him, but he didn't look back.

That night, in bed with his mother's picture under his pillow, Nicholas felt overwhelmed with a mixture of shame and embarrassment. He had made a fool of himself. Ellie would probably never have anything more to do with him.

• • •

When Maggie was helping Pa with the milking, she told him about running into Nicholas on the prairie.

"I thought the Ebenezers were poor, Pa," she said. "Asa and Cora always look poor. But they've got more cattle than we have."

"Havin' a few cows don't mean you're rich, lassie," said Pa. "It just means you've got cows. Newt Ebenezer is as poor as anyone in this district. There's no shame, though, in being

73

poor. Many have bad luck. This is a hard country and only some get on. Newt's a good worker, but a poor manager, I figure. And he's hard on everyone. Treats his animals bad, and his family not much better. Come to think of it, it's hard to figure just how poor he is, because he's so mean. He pinches a penny 'til it squeals."

Mother had come into the barn while Pa was talking. "Newt Ebenezer's so mean he'd skin a flea for the hide and tallow," she said as she filled a bucket with grain for her chickens.

Chapter Twelve

A Challenge

Miss Fieldmont raised her pitch pipe to her lips. She saw the little children directly in front of her, all with their mouths open like baby birds waiting for worms. Asa Ebenezer, the big boy in the back seat, raised his hand and she lowered her pitch pipe.

"Please, Miss," said Asa, "why do we have to learn music? My dad says all we need to learn is to read and write and do sums."

Miss Fieldmont smiled a little. The big boys looked knowingly at each other as if the smile meant that she was soft after all. Miss Fieldmont saw the look and stopped smiling.

"Of course you need arithmetic and reading, Asa. But music is something special. When we raise our voices, we raise our spirits. And we join in spirit with others around the world who sing the same songs. Music is an important part of our civilization, Asa, and we are bringing civilization to this new land." Miss Fieldmont felt a little flushed with the earnestness of her speech.

Asa looked at his mates with a "Didn't I tell you?" expression. His grin was open now. He leaned back and hooked his thumbs in his suspenders. Five other big boys in the back rows all leaned back and hooked their thumbs in their suspenders. Miss Fieldmont stiffened. The little children were ashen.

"An important part of our what, Miss Field Mouse? I don't figure I know what you're talkin' about, Miss Field Mouse."

Miss Fieldmont opened her drawer and took out the strap. Her hands were shaking, so she clenched her fists, drew herself up to her full height and said in a firm voice, "Asa, come to the front of the room."

Asa stood up, his grin really dazzling now. He turned his head to his mates in what was nearly a bow, then he ambled toward her, swinging his shoulders as he came.

Miss Fieldmont's toe was tapping the floor, almost imperceptibly under her long skirt. "Asa, I am your teacher. You must mind me and show respect if you are to learn. I will give you six on each hand."

He put out his hand and she swung with all her might. The strap came through the air with a whoosh and there was a cracking sound as it hit his palm. He grinned. By the time she swung for the sixth time, Asa's palm was red and the grin gone.

"Now, Asa," she said, panting a little, "the other hand."

Asa glanced at the other students, all sitting upright now, leaning forward a little. Most of the little ones were sitting on their hands.

"Asa!"

He held out his hand. Miss Fieldmont had regained her breath, and the stroke was as hard as the first. At the second stroke, he pulled his hand back so that the strap caught just the tips of his fingers. She paused and said firmly, "Pulling back doubles it. Now you get twelve."

She resumed hitting, though her arm was getting tired. Asa's face became flushed, his eyes grew moist and his lips began to twitch. The tears began while she was on the last six, and when she let him take his seat he put his head down on his arms.

"Asa," she said, her voice small and tired, "we have to work together to make this a good school. I expect you will do your duty. I promise I will do mine."

Maggie was shaken by this tableau. She was glad to see the school was going to be controlled by the teacher rather than the bullies, but she had never before seen anyone struck by a teacher, and it upset her. In her school in Fredericton, a disruptive student like Asa would have been sent to the principal's office, and maybe to the guidance counsellor. She realized there was no principal for Miss Fieldmont to turn to. And she also realized that, if Miss Fieldmont had turned to someone outside the school for help, like the school board, she would have never gained the students' respect. Or that of the parents.

· · ·

The week skimmed by on the strength of Miss Fieldmont's victory. Now that the boys saw she wasn't soft, after all, they were quiet and respectful, but only when the teacher was in the room. Asa, Bert and the others were still mean when she wasn't watching. But things were so much better, Maggie looked forward to each day, and was making headway in teaching Cora to read.

At the end of the week, Maggie was driving home with the teacher. Penny and Copper were stepping along, and Maggie was proudly in the driver's seat. As they drew near home, she could see that Mother was cleaning a freshly killed chicken. There was a smear of red on her cheek where she'd brushed away a fly. The sleeves of her faded print dress were rolled up, showing her strong, sinewy arms.

Mother looked up. "I'll be going in to get your supper in a minute, Miss. You look to your horses, then go and dig some potatoes and get them peeled, Ellie. Now don't dawdle! I want to get this chicken cooked tomorrow so we can make sandwiches for Sunday tea. We'll need lots of food — I expect there'll be a lot of 'em coming over, your first Sunday tea and all."

"Oh? Who?" Miss Fieldmont raised her eyebrows.

"Why, young men. There aren't many spinster ladies in a place like this. They'll come along on a Sunday pretending to visit the neighbours, but really they'll be here to meet you."

"Oh," said Miss Fieldmont in a tone of faint enthusiasm, "what a quaint custom."

Friday night and Saturday passed in a whirl of energetic preparations for Sunday. Maggie and Mother cooked and cleaned while Miss Fieldmont, somewhat reluctantly, entered into the spirit of the proceedings. She pressed her pretty wine-coloured dress, polished her grey kid boots, and washed her dark hair with rose-scented soap in the big china washbowl Mother had bought for her in Valhalla. Maggie's little tin basin was in her new room, the lean-to at the end of the house.

After the noon meal on Sunday, Miss Fieldmont lit a coal oil lamp and heated a curling iron in the lamp chimney. When it was hot she curled her bangs and frizzed them out with her fingers. Then she tore a petal from a cloth rose, wet it and rubbed it on her cheeks until some of the colour was transferred off. She looked lovely with her pink cheeks and deep hazel eyes.

At three o'clock, two rigs pulled into the yard. While the drivers were tethering their horses in the poplar bluff behind the house, a third rig arrived.

The first to come to the door was Mr. Karlson. He was dressed in a flannel shirt and heavy worsted trousers. His face reddened and he couldn't seem to bring himself to look at Miss Fieldmont. When introduced to her he mumbled something in the direction of the worn board floor, which was bleached nearly white from Mother's hard scrubbing and lye soap.

The next visitor was Mr. Phillips-Jones. He was tall, slim and very handsome, with shiny black hair slicked back from his face. He was elegantly dressed in a well-cut suit with a silk double-breasted waistcoat and he wore a smart wool fedora. He spoke with an English accent and, when introduced, he bowed over Miss Fieldmont's hand in a charming manner. Miss Fieldmont smiled.

Maggie opened the door for the last caller, Mr. Trent. Pa said he didn't know what to make of all those books Trent read, but he was honest and a good neighbour.

"How do you do, Miss Trenholme," Mr. Trent said with exaggerated formality as he shook Maggie's hand. Maggie couldn't help laughing. He wore a well-brushed dark suit with a shirt so sparkling white it rivalled his smile. But, next to Mr. Phillips-Jones, he looked a little rough, a little out of style. His face was honest and pleasant, with a craggy brow and intense blue eyes. When he shook hands with Miss Fieldmont, Maggie saw her cold look, and realized the teacher was still thinking of Mr. Trent's ill-considered offer to help her do her job.

Pa ushered them to the table. Mother poured tea and began passing around chicken sandwiches, scones with chokecherry jelly, and saskatoon tarts. The gentlemen all ate steadily and nearly silently. Their teeth were stained blue by the juicy little berries in the tarts. Only when they could eat no more did they seem to relax and lean back in their chairs.

While they sipped their tea, Maggie noticed that Mr. Karlson's and Mr. Trent's hands were calloused and rough, with broken fingernails like Pa's, while Mr. Phillips-Jones' hands were soft and pink and his nails were neatly filed.

Miss Fieldmont cleared her throat. "By your accent, Mr. Phillips-Jones, I judge you have not been in Canada long."

"You are correct, Miss. I came from England to take up a homestead."

"How is your crop?" asked Pa, politely.

"Fair, fair," the elegant man answered, turning away from the teacher. "But, with all the setbacks of the last few years, I don't know how I'd manage without help from my family in the Old Country. And the field-workers available for hire in this area, why they're quite lazy and incompetent." He turned again toward Miss Fieldmont. "But someday my farm will be a showplace. I can guarantee that!"

Miss Fieldmont turned to Mr. Trent. "And you, sir. Have you lived here long?"

"Oh, going on about four years," he drawled. "I came from Ontario when my folks passed away. We had fifty acres of stones to farm there and could barely feed ourselves. I knew as soon as I saw the land around here that this is where a man, and a woman too," he said, looking levelly at her, "has a future. If you work hard, there's no limit to what you can do."

Miss Fieldmont did something which surprised Maggie. She blushed.

While Mr. Trent was talking, Mr. Karlson was looking more and more terrified. His face reddened and his hand shook so that his cup rattled in the saucer. He turned to Pa and began asking, almost desperately, about his crop. The men were all soon deep in conversation, leaving Miss Fieldmont, Maggie and Mother helplessly on the sidelines, occasionally refilling the cups, but outsiders nonetheless.

Maggie tuned into the conversation when she heard Dan Trent refer to some strange goings-on in the community.

"It's happened twice over the last three or four weeks," he said. "An animal disappears, and the farmer finds its" — he looked at Mother and Miss Fieldmont before choosing the next word — "its insides lying on the ground in the pasture. Someone is coming into a pasture when no one's about and butchering beef right there, then hauling off the carcass. Nobody seems to be able to figure out what's going on."

"It sure is a mystery," said Pa. "I've known of cattle thieves before, but never heard tell of butcherin' the beef right under the farmer's nose. Makes the stealin' more despicable, somehow."

The men talked on for another half-hour. If they had looked at Miss Fieldmont, they would have seen the storm signals, but it seemed they were more interested in discussing an expensive team of horses that a neighbour had bought from a homesteader who'd been beaten by the prairies and had gone back to Ontario.

"Well, just look at the time," said Mr. Trent, pulling out his pocket watch and glancing at it. "I must be heading home." Miss Fieldmont looked surprised.

As he was leaving, Mr. Phillips-Jones turned to Mother. "Thank you ever so much for the delicious tea. May I ask if the teacher prepared any of it — the tarts perhaps? The scones?"

"No, not this time, this being her first few days here and all."

"Then," broke in Mr. Trent, "perhaps we'll be able to sample her cooking next week." He shook hands with Mother and thanked her for the wonderful lunch. Mr. Karlson engaged the floor in a moment of mumbled conversation before bolting for the door.

When they were gone, Mother turned to Miss Fieldmont, who had her hands on her hips and was tapping the floor with the toe of her little grey boot, ominously.

"Don't be cross with them, Miss," Mother said. "Food is very important to these men who work so hard. They can fry meat and potatoes, but they're not much on baking, and they get hungry for it."

"But they barely spoke to me," hissed Miss Fieldmont.

Mother said firmly, glad of a chance to offer advice, "I've a notion they think it isn't seemly for a well-brought-up young lady like yourself to just go talking to a man. They're waiting 'til they get to know you better."

"How do they expect to get to know me better if they don't speak to me?" Miss Fieldmont's voice was rising a little with each distinctly pronounced word.

Mother looked at her as if she was slow-witted. "Why, by eating your cooking, of course!"

• • •

The next morning, on the way to school, Maggie screwed up her courage and asked, "Miss Fieldmont, would you like to have a beau?"

Miss Fieldmont looked intently at her for a moment, then she spoke. "Don't tell anyone, Ellie, not even your mother. But yes, I'd like to meet a young man. Someone to take me dancing — and to church on Sunday mornings. But I have very high standards. He'd have to be well educated, and have good manners and be well dressed. But, above all, he must not think that women can't understand anything beyond cooking and cleaning!"

Maggie was very interested in Miss Fieldmont's opinion. Mother wouldn't have agreed. She had told Maggie that Miss Fieldmont shouldn't be too fussy in choosing a beau. If she was, she ran the chance of dying a lonely old maid. It seemed to Maggie that Miss Fieldmont would find that fate preferable to settling for less than the best. Miss Fieldmont smiled at Maggie, and Maggie smiled back.

Then Maggie asked, "Do you think you will choose one of the Sunday callers to be your beau?"

Miss Fieldmont looked thoughtful. "Mr. Phillips-Jones seems to be the only possibility. He is educated ... and he dresses very well. In England, where he comes from, I think they are more used to treating women like equals than they are here in this rough country."

Then her voice got quite chilly. "Mr. Trent doesn't have any idea how to treat a lady. And poor Mr. Karlson! I do believe if I said so much as boo to him, he'd fall down in a fit of apoplexy!"

They both chuckled at that image of Mr. Karlson. Then, because the fall sun was warm on their cheeks and their spirits were high, their laughter peeled across the prairie. A gopher poked its head out of its hole and gave them a quizzical look.

"None of them has real manners," continued Miss Fieldmont. "Oh, Mr. Phillips-Jones thinks he has, but they all acted in a high-handed way, Ellie. I just wish I could think of a way to teach them that they can't get away with treating a modern woman as if she had nothing to say worth hearing ... as if she were invisible!"

They trudged on in silence. Suddenly Miss Fieldmont stopped stock still. She stared at Maggie a few moments, then she said, "Yes, that's it! If what the settlers around here are looking for is someone to cook for them, then I'll feed them some cooking they'll never forget!"

Chapter Thirteen

Secret Meetings

Mornings were chilly now, and Mother kept the fire going after breakfast was cooked. The poplars had lost most of their yellow leaves. A golden spray floated to the ground whenever a breeze sprang up. Some were already bare, looking like skeletons against the sky. Pa looked out each morning to check the weather, to see if it looked like snow. Most of the threshing in the district was finished, and Pa said he'd worry about his crop until it was safe in the bin.

"I don't know what we'll do if we lose even part of the crop," he fussed. "We've got nothing else to fall back on, now that we spent all our savings on a team of horses." He looked at Mother when he said this. Maggie knew he loved Penny and Copper as much as she did, but he was truly worried.

"Don't fret over what you can't change, Pa," Mother scolded. "The threshers are over at Mr. Trent's now, and you know how much land he has! They'll get here when they can!"

Every day, after school, Maggie rode either Penny or Copper out on the prairie. She had several hours of lessons to memorize each night because Miss Fieldmont was preparing her to write the entrance examinations to high school in Valhalla next year. She would be the first student from Victoria to write the exams.

Mother and Pa didn't know how they would pay for room and board for their daughter in town. Valhalla was five miles away, too far for her to drive night and morning in winter. But Mother said, "We'll cross that bridge when we come to it. The Lord helps those who help themselves. The first thing you can do to help yourself, Ellie, is pass those exams."

So both parents agreed that she could study on the prairie while she was herding the cattle. Miss Fieldmont dug some textbooks out of one of her trunks for Maggie to study geometry, algebra and Latin. Maggie had never learned Latin in her school in Fredericton, but she had studied French grammar, and that helped. Grammar seemed like a jigsaw puzzle to her, with all the pieces of sentences neatly fitting into their proper slots.

Every day, she met Nicholas on the prairie. He seemed frightened of riding, so Maggie didn't press him. She did encourage him to get to know her horses. He was reluctant to approach them, but if she held their heads he would reach out and pat their faces or rub their necks. He would stand as far away as possible and lean forward on his toes. Maggie thought this was strange behaviour, but she didn't comment.

Every day Nicholas read from the book of myths. His favourite story was the one about Pegasus, a winged horse. He read that one over and over.

While he read, he munched food Maggie brought for him. They milked a little into a pan she brought and he drank deeply of the warm, rich milk. They knew that if they milked only one cow, someone might notice how little it gave at milking time, so they milked a little out of several cows.

Nicholas was getting stronger every day. His face was tanned and had lost its pale, city look.

When Maggie and Nicholas weren't studying or chasing the cows, she told him what was happening at school and in the community. Some days he seemed preoccupied. He moved slowly, and there was a pinched look on his face. On those days, she suspected he had been beaten again.

"I'm going to tell people how that horrible Newt Ebenezer beats you," she said. "It's so unfair!"

"That wouldn't do any good," said Nicholas. "People would just say that I get what I deserve. They'd turn against me even more."

He was quiet for a moment, and when he spoke again his voice had a steely quality. "I'll get away, someday," he said. "But someday isn't now. So, I put the bad to the back of my mind and think of the good. And the good is having you for a friend, and reading the book."

Nicholas looked into Maggie's eyes. "Promise you won't tell?"

For a moment, Maggie felt she couldn't promise any such thing. Then she remembered how Mother and Pa had reacted when she told them about the bullies at school. Maybe Nicholas was right. Telling wouldn't do any good. Pa and Mother would probably think that Mr. Ebenezer was disciplining the boy just as Miss Fieldmont had disciplined Asa when she gave him the strap. Nicholas was still looking at her with a quiet, forceful gaze. Finally she said, "I promise."

One day Nicholas looked particularly downcast. He had found out that, once the harvest was done, the cows could run free. Then he would be spending his days helping Newt Ebenezer build a cattle shed. A pile of logs was already drying in the farmyard.

"I don't think we'll ever see each other again!" Nicholas said angrily.

"We won't let that happen," said Maggie brightly, with more conviction than she felt. "We'll find ways. I'm sure of it."

That night, Maggie told Miss Fieldmont, casually, that she had seen Nicholas on the prairie. She didn't want anyone to know that they met regularly in case it got back to the Ebenezers.

She informed the teacher that Nicholas had been told that a Home Inspector would come out on the train periodically to make sure the terms of the agreement were being met. But, so far, no inspector had arrived.

Miss Fieldmont said, "Well, we'll have to see about this! I'll write Winnipeg right away and report that a Home Child is not attending school. That should get an inspector out here."

One Saturday, Maggie had to leave Nicholas on the prairie at noon, because she was going into Valhalla with Mother. Pa was working with the threshers. They had been threshing at Mr. Phillips-Jones' for several days, since he had the biggest farm in the district.

Nicholas looked so disappointed when she said she was leaving that she almost told him she would stay, but she quickly changed her mind. She was anxious to see what town was like. She missed stores and crowds.

Back at the house, she only had time to change into her school dress, grab a snack and jump into the buggy with Mother. They had to hurry to be back in time for milking.

When they drove into Valhalla, Maggie was very excited. A town. A real town!

There was one long main street. Some of the buildings had high square fronts hiding low buildings behind, like those she had seen in western movies. But there were also big square frame buildings of two or three storeys, and, on the corner, a new, three-storey building built of bricks. Since the streets were wide, the land flat, and there were no trees of any size, as they drove down the street she could get a sense of the whole town.

Clearly visible, a block away, was the railway station, with its wide platform by the tracks. Beyond that were two high buildings, like awkward towers, with no windows but with ramps leading up to big double doors. One of the buildings had "VALHALLA" in big letters on it. She had never seen anything like it. There were five or six farmers driving wagons heaped with sacks of grain up the ramps. Then she realized what they were. These huge frame constructions looming against the prairie sky were grain elevators.

Mother found room at a hitching rail for Penny and Copper. Maggie climbed down and looped the halter ropes over the rail. They were in front of the new brick building. It had big plate-glass windows and there were two sets of double doors. Above one set was a sign saying *Candle Brothers' General Store*. In the store window were signs advertising Fels Naphtha soap and Dutch Cleanser. Above the other door, the sign read *Butcher's Shop — Fresh and Cured Meats*. Mother took a basket of butter out of the buggy. She was going to trade it for groceries she needed. Today it would be for sugar, coffee and corn syrup.

Maggie asked to walk around a little, and Mother told her to meet her in an hour at Kwan's Confectionery. So Maggie had a whole hour in which to explore!

The town was bustling. The wide dusty streets were full of wagons and buggies, but only a few people were on horseback. There were planks laid down either side of the street so pedestrians could keep out of the dust. Maggie was amazed at the range of stores. There were real estate offices, a bank and a farm-implement store with binders and ploughs lined up at the side. There was a huge unpainted three-storey building with the single word *Hotel* painted across grey weathered boards. Next door was another large building, but only one storey. Her nose told her what it was before she read the sign: *Livery Stable*. Beside the door was a huge manure pile.

She turned down a side street and passed a brick house with a sign by the front door: *Dr. Peters, Physician and Surgeon.* A beautiful bay horse was tethered beside it. Farther along were some small houses, each with a single cow grazing in the backyard. At the back of each lot was an animal shed and an outdoor toilet.

She turned onto another street and marvelled at a few big frame houses, painted cream or brown or dark green. Some had fancy verandas and big windows. One had a curving brick walk and one had a gazebo. The fenced yards were landscaped with flower beds and small trees, recently planted. These homes were much fancier than any she'd seen since she'd come to Manitoba.

On another street, there were more businesses with signs advertising everything from bicycles to sewing machines. One sign caught her eye. It said *Fridbjorn Jonsson Harness and Boot Shop.* The front door was propped open, and she glanced into the dim interior. She jumped a little as a tennis ball bounced out the door. She easily caught it and waited for the owner to appear. In a moment a girl about her age dashed out the door, laughing. The girl had light brown hair with golden strands shining where the sun hit it. Her dress was short enough to show off white stockings knit in an intricate pattern and smooth brown leather boots with black toes. Oh, how Maggie wished she had boots like that! Everything the girl wore had a fashionable "store bought" look. Maggie was envious only for a moment, then she felt ashamed of herself. Mother had worked hard to make her clothes, and they were as nice as any worn by country girls.

She handed the girl the ball and started walking away when the girl said, "Ellie? It's Ellie Trenholme, isn't it?"

"Yes?" said Maggie, hesitantly.

"We met last year at your school when our class was invited for Field Day. My name is Kristjana. Don't you remember me?"

Maggie had learned when to pretend knowledge of things Ellie would know, and when to admit ignorance. She shook her head.

"Well," said Kristjana, "I remember you. You were the one who was nice enough to stand up for me when all those horrible boys were making fun of my Icelandic accent. I told you then that I would never forget you, and I haven't!"

Maggie felt a little thrill. She had just learned something more about the kind of person Ellie was. She was glad it was something good.

Before she knew what was happening, Kristjana was leading her through the shop to some stairs at the back. They paused a moment for Kristjana to introduce her father.

"I know your father well," he said to Maggie. "You're welcome here anytime."

Kristjana took Maggie up the stairs at the back of the shop. At the top was a landing, with a door on the left and a door on the right. "This way is our home," said Kristjana, leading Maggie into an apartment.

"What's through the other door?" Maggie asked, pointing across the landing.

"Empty rooms," said Kristjana. "Father wants to rent them, but so far they're empty."

Kristjana's apartment was small and simply furnished, but everything was shining clean and neat. Kristjana showed Maggie shelves of books in the living room. Some were written in Icelandic, but many were in English. There was a picture on the wall of a pretty woman.

"My mother," said Kristjana. "Her name was Sigridur. Isn't that the prettiest name? Someday, when I have a daughter, I'll name her Sigridur."

"Her name *was* Sigridur. You mean ..."

"She died last year."

"Who looks after you?"

"My father. But he says I look after him. I do most of the cooking and cleaning because he must work long hours, sometimes until late at night. He says we mustn't complain. Long hours means he has built up a good business. But I worry about his health. He works too hard." Then she repeated, "I worry about his health ..."

Kristjana's voice trailed away, but Maggie understood. Kristjana didn't want anything to happen to the only parent she had left.

Kristjana took her to her bedroom and showed her the dolls she had played with when she was younger. They were all neatly lined up on a dresser.

The girls sat on the bed, looked at the dolls and giggled about games they had played when they were small. Suddenly Maggie realized how long she had been there. If she was late meeting Mother, she would be in trouble.

She had to run all the way to Kwan's Confectionery. But when she got there, Mother was sitting at a table in the back of the store, sipping coffee. She looked very severe in her best black dress with her hair pulled into a tight bun, but when she saw Maggie she patted the seat of the chair beside her. Then she ordered ice cream for a special treat.

The ice cream was served by an old Chinese lady, dressed head to toe in black. She seemed to understand everything Mother said, but she didn't speak back, she only smiled. Maggie heard her talking in Chinese to the young man behind the counter, probably her son. The people at the next table were speaking French. In just an hour in Valhalla, she had heard three languages other than English.

"Mother," she asked, "why don't we hear people speaking other languages at Victoria?"

"Because almost everyone out our way comes from Ontario. Oh, a few are from Scotland or England. Some from Quebec and the Maritimes. But most came from Ontario.

"The Icelanders settled north of here in their own communities. Like us, they come to Valhalla to do their business. Those French-speaking people are from east of here. They sometimes come to shop, but it's a long way from where they live." Mother paused and took a sip of her coffee, then she went on.

"I can tell you one thing about every one of the settlers in Manitoba, Ellie. They all came from somewheres worse. Most, like us, came from small hard farms full of stones and covered with trees that had to be cut down one by one to get a bit more land to grow a bit more grain. It was a hopeless life that sapped our strength."

"Why did the Icelanders come?" asked Maggie.

"I heard that they was worse off than most of us. Near starvation back in Iceland. Volcanoes erupting with fire and brimstone that killed their sheep. Oh, it's hard to imagine!"

"Pa says this is a hard country," said Maggie.

Mother was looking at her, but it seemed as though she was looking through her. She was so caught up in explaining that she ignored Maggie and went on with her story.

"This new country, with its homesteads for the asking, its big open fields just waiting to be planted, why it seemed like the Garden of Eden to us settlers. Those early months, when we first came," she added grimly, "we didn't know what a Manitoba winter was, and no one had told us about prairie fires and hail and droughts." She paused to sip her coffee.

"But not many of us have given up," Mother went on. "Now, the worst is behind us and people are beginning to prosper. Manitoba truly is the land of opportunity, just like we thought when we came here. Don't ever believe different, child."

As she said this she was gazing out the window at all the fine horses lined up at the hitching rail, and there was a light of pride in her eyes. She sighed and drained her cup and set it down on the saucer with a determined thunk, as if she were coming back to earth.

"Now, Ellie," she said, "hurry and finish that ice cream. We've got to get home quickly and get some baking laid away. The teacher's suitors are coming tomorrow, and we should start getting ready for the threshers. Pa says they might be here as early as Monday. You won't be going to school for a few days. I can't do everything by myself."

Maggie was silent on the way home. She was thinking of Kristjana and wishing she could see her again. She wanted to ask her about what terrible things had driven the Icelanders out of their own country. But she wanted to see Kristjana for more than that. She wanted a friend. She hadn't realized until this afternoon just how terribly she missed Colleen.

Chapter Fourteen

The Sunday Callers

That evening, Maggie was sitting at the table darning Pa's work socks. Miss Fieldmont came up behind Mother as she was fluting the edges of a pumpkin pie with deft little movements of fingers and thumb. "Mrs. Trenholme, will you let me bake something while you sit down and have a cup of tea?"

Mother looked sceptically at the teacher as she popped the pie into the oven of the big black cast-iron stove. "I could use a little rest. Do you want a recipe?"

"No. I'm quite used to it — my aunt trained me, and I can remember my mother teaching me, though she died when I was only ten."

Mother poured water into the teapot from a kettle always kept simmering on the stove, then pulled up a chair to the table. "Hard. Life is hard." She sighed. "And your father?"

"They both died of typhus — within a week of each other. I went to an aunt and uncle who owned a successful business

— a department store in a nearby town. I was very lucky. They treated me like their own and always gave me the best of everything. My brother went to another uncle on a little farm, as poor and heartbreaking as our parents' farm was."

Mother sighed as she sipped her tea. Maggie felt a great rush of sadness. She wanted to tell Miss Fieldmont that she understood, because her father had died when she was a baby and her mother had died when she was only six. But, of course, she could say nothing of the kind. Miss Fieldmont just closed her eyes for a moment, then went on with her baking.

"Why did you come to teach here — so far from home?" asked Maggie.

"Oh, my aunt and uncle expected me to teach in the best schools of Halifax or Fredericton. But I chose the prairies because … because everything is new." She turned to the window and gazed across the prairie. "I can help build a new society here. There is challenge here, Ellie. I can never turn away from a challenge." She put a lump of butter in the bowl, took the cracked cup with no handle that was used to measure, dipped it into the crock marked "SALT" and raised it heaping full, then poured it over the butter and began to cream the two.

"Oh my soul!" said Mother, startled. "You've gone and put in a cupful of the salt instead of the sugar!"

Miss Fieldmont smiled slyly and kept on stirring. "I'm going to make a raisin cake for the gentlemen the like of which they've never had before," she said.

All the preparations had to be done on Saturday, because on Sunday only two activities were allowed in this pioneer community. In the morning, the whole family would dress in their best and go to church. The sermon was long and boring, but Maggie liked seeing their neighbours and what kind of horses they drove. In the afternoon, people would call on neighbours, where they expected to be fed a liberal afternoon lunch. Or, they would stay at home, resting from their week's hard labour, with the cupboards full of food, waiting for someone to call.

Sunday afternoon, within a few minutes of one another, three rigs pulled into the Trenholmes' yard and disappeared into the poplar bluff behind the house. Mr. Phillips-Jones appeared at the door, his moustache waxed to needle points, with a bouquet of wildflowers, which he presented to Miss Fieldmont with a sweeping bow. She looked even more attractive than usual today in a white-sprigged blue dress with a tight-fitting bodice. She coloured a little and looked pleased at the gift.

Mr. Trent shook hands all round, then headed for the table without another word. Miss Fieldmont looked disgruntled. Mr. Karlson appeared a few minutes later with a startling haircut. His face and neck were burned red by the prairie sun and wind. Obviously, he was one of those practical men who ask that their hair be cut short enough to last for several months, and as a result he had a band of white skin about his neck and ears which reminded Maggie of pictures of soldiers with bandages wound round their heads. She could see Miss Fieldmont biting her lip and a little muscle twitching in her cheek. Mother poured the tea and passed around roast-beef sandwiches.

"Well, gentlemen," said Miss Fieldmont, speaking out boldly, "tell me, what do you think of the Prime Minister?" All eyes turned toward her and there was utter silence. "The Prime Minister of Canada," she repeated, "what do you think of his policies? His political skill?"

Mr. Karlson's open mouth snapped shut with an audible clicking of teeth. He stared into his plate. Mr. Trent flashed his sparkling smile. Was he laughing at her?

"Tell me, Miss Fieldmont," he said quietly, "which prime minister are you referring to? We seem to have a new one every ten minutes ever since Sir John A. went to his reward. Now, if you want to discuss a fine prime minister, let's discuss Sir John A. Macdonald."

The suave Mr. Phillips-Jones said icily, "That's not a topic to discuss with a lady, Trent. Politics is a dirty business."

Miss Fieldmont offered Mr. Phillips-Jones such a beaming smile that he preened and flicked the ends of his moustache with the back of his hand.

"I consider your attitude gallant," she said sweetly, then her voice took on a steely note, "but old-fashioned. I was on the debating team at the Ladies' Academy in New Brunswick. I happen to like politics."

"Well, I don't consider such concerns ladylike," said Phillips-Jones, as if his opinion was the only one that mattered. "Don't worry your genteel little head over such things," he said to Miss Fieldmont. "A true gentleman" — and he looked scathingly at Mr. Trent — "never discusses unpleasant topics with a lady."

"But we discuss things like that in school," said Maggie. "We have a new subject now called Current Events."

Mr. Phillips-Jones, who was seated next to her, looked down his nose at Maggie. "I thought children were meant to be seen and not heard," he said.

Maggie felt her face getting hot. She looked at Pa, but he was shaking his head gently at her.

As if to relieve the tension, Mr. Phillips-Jones said to Miss Fieldmont, "Tell me, did you bake any of this wonderful food?"

Just then Pa reached for the cake and, to his amazement, just as his fingers grazed a piece, Miss Fieldmont snatched it from his reach. It did look tempting, with plump raisins protruding from it, and covered with a thick layer of boiled, brown-sugar icing. She held it in front of Mr. Phillips-Jones.

"I do so hope you will enjoy it," she purred. "I made it all by myself, and I would like you to have the first piece!"

Mr. Phillips-Jones, whose manners were refined, broke a small piece from the edge of his cake, and tucked it under his moustache with the air of a connoisseur. His expression changed from anticipation to surprise, then to horror, as he dove for his cup, drained it, then held it out speechlessly to Mother. She refilled it without comment, a tiny smile tugging at the corners of her mouth.

Everyone was staring at Mr. Phillips-Jones' little pantomime but Mr. Karlson, who hadn't dared look up from his plate for some time. Now all eyes turned to him as he, glance still downcast, took in a whole square of cake in one enormous bite. His jaws worked steadily for a moment, then they froze. His eyes seemed to start from his head, then they began to water. His cheeks bulged with unswallowed cake. His hands fluttered helplessly near his mouth, as if they wanted to rescue his tongue. The poor man, in a final fit of agony, dove for the door, sending his chair clattering backward on the floor in the process. They could hear him spitting and sputtering outside.

Pa half raised himself from his chair with a muttered "What's going —?" but at a signal from Mother sat down again. As they listened to Mr. Karlson's horse galloping out of the yard, Mr. Phillips-Jones thanked Mother, then made his escape.

Four pairs of eyes turned to Mr. Trent. He glanced at Mr. Karlson's empty plate, and at the uneaten cake on Mr. Phillips-Jones' plate. Then he slowly raised his piece to his lips, gazing directly at Miss Fieldmont as he did so. He bit off a piece and chewed it thoughtfully. He swallowed, with only the slightest hesitation, then bit again. He repeated the procedure again and again, until his cake was gone. Only then did he pass his cup for more tea.

"Tell me," he said, smiling at Miss Fieldmont, "do you debate as well as you cook?" She didn't answer but there was a slight twitch beside her mouth.

"To return to the discussion that so offended our gentleman friend," he said with just the slightest note of sarcasm. "Miss Fieldmont, what do you think of Canada's first and finest prime minister?"

"I think Mr. Macdonald was insensitive and indecisive," she answered. "Just look at how he mishandled the language question in the Manitoba schools."

"Mishandled, nothing!" he said heatedly, leaning toward her. "If he'd lived long enough, he would have settled the issue to everyone's satisfaction."

"Ah, my dear Mr. Trent, Mr. Macdonald did nothing to quell the flames of bigotry. He decided to hang Riel. He set the stage for hard feelings between the French and the English in this country for generations to come. You mark my words."

"I don't think Riel should have been hanged any more than you do," said Mr. Trent. "But don't blame Macdonald. He was forced into it by rich and powerful interests — people who care nothing about justice for the poor and weak."

"Now you're making excuses for him," began Miss Fieldmont. Then she paused, as if she had only then realized the effect she was having on the others around the table. Maggie was leaning forward, soaking up every word. Mother was sipping tea and looking like the cat that got the cream. And Pa — why, Pa was the picture of confusion. His neighbours, men he had always considered sane, had rushed from his table as if pursued by the devil. And this slight young lady was arguing politics as if she were a man!

"Miss Fieldmont," said Mr. Trent, "there's to be a dance at the school Saturday night. With any luck we should be finished threshing by then. Would you do me the honour of letting me escort you?"

"Why, thank you, Mr. Trent," she replied in a matter-of-fact voice. "I will be pleased to attend the dance with you. Would you like me to bake something to bring along for lunch?" she asked sweetly, as an afterthought, her eyebrows raised.

"Please, no!" he said with exaggerated urgency. "There's no need." Then he flashed his smile. "But I'd be grateful if we continued our debate along the way. I always enjoy an intelligent conversation with someone who holds such strong opinions."

"A debate then," she said. "I do enjoy a challenge."

"I look forward to Saturday," said Mr. Trent. "But right now I have a powerful hankering for another cup of tea!"

As Maggie filled his cup, she caught Miss Fieldmont's eye, and they grinned at each other over the teapot. Dan Trent started to chuckle, softly at first. Miss Fieldmont joined in, then Maggie giggled and Mother's shoulders began to tremble. Soon they were all laughing hysterically, except for Pa, who sat shaking his head, trying to figure out what was so funny.

When Mr. Trent had gone, there was a knock on the door. When Pa opened it, they were all surprised to see Mr. Phillips-Jones standing there. He looked a little crestfallen, with his hat in his hand. Mother suddenly became very busy clearing the table, while Pa went to the stove and started digging in the firebox with the poker. Miss Fieldmont slowly walked toward the door and stood with one hand on her hip, as Maggie had seen her stand while she waited for the class to settle down.

Mr. Phillips-Jones bowed his head. "Now that I've eaten a piece of your cake," he said seriously, "or was it humble pie? I was wondering if you have it in your heart to forgive me. It was obvious that something I said offended you, and for that I'm truly sorry."

There was a moment of silence, then Miss Fieldmont smiled up into his handsome face. "I accept your apology," she said.

Mr. Phillips-Jones relaxed visibly. He tugged his shirt cuffs so they showed beneath his cuffs, and he smiled. "You are very kind! Can I dare to hope you will be kind enough to attend the dance on Saturday with me?"

Maggie was at the table washing the dishes, but when she heard this she looked at Miss Fieldmont. The teacher seemed startled.

"I'm sorry," she said, "I've already agreed to go to the dance with Mr. Trent."

Maggie saw Mr. Phillips-Jones clench his fists for a moment, but he quickly hid his feelings. "Then, could I escort you to church next week?" he asked.

"That's a very kind invitation," said Miss Fieldmont cheerfully. "I'd be happy to go to church on your arm."

Mr. Phillips-Jones smiled, bowed and took his leave. Miss Fieldmont turned from the door, her eyes sparkling. She hummed a cheerful little tune under her breath as she went to her room. Through the open door, Maggie could see her taking two full-skirted gowns out of a trunk and spreading them on the bed.

"Choices, choices!" Miss Fieldmont sang out happily. "It's always nice to have a choice." Then she burst into song.

> *Down yonder green valley*
> *Where streamlets meander*
> *I first met my dear one*
> *Down by the ash grove*

Chapter Fifteen

The Threshing Gang

"Pa's like a cat on a hot griddle, he's so excited," Mother said. Maggie could feel the excitement in the morning air as she and Mother stood by the window and watched the threshers coming down the lane.

The huge steam engine pulled into the yard like an iron dinosaur and trundled slowly, snorting all the way, through the barnyard and out to Pa's wheat field beyond. Behind it were the marks of its giant wheels, the lugs cutting into the black soil like the footprints of a monster from another world. Then came the oddest-looking machine of all, the separator, with a long-nosed pipe on the side and a white canvas conveyor of some kind, with wooden slats like ladder steps. Following in the strange parade was a wagon loaded with barrels for water, and wagons with men riding, holding their pitchforks like walking-sticks.

Mother stood at the window and watched, brushing sweat off her forehead with her sleeve. The last few days had been unusually hot for the fall, hot as summer. The iron cookstove was red and smoking, and steam filled the air. Mother and Maggie had started cooking early. They had to feed the gang of men who had come to thresh, and, Mother said, they had a reputation to live up to for setting the best table in the district.

"The men complain of the stingy ways of Matilda Ebenezer," said Mother. "They got only one kind of pie there. And it was sour. And the crust nearly broke their teeth. And no cake. Poor soul, she doesn't have much to work with. There are other farms where they say the keep is poor. But not here! I pride myself on setting a good table. Now, this year, Ellie, we have to outdo ourselves!"

"Why?" asked Maggie. She was peeling potatoes from a big basin and there was a pailful nearby to peel when these were finished.

"Because when the threshers were at Dan Trent's, they said they got the best food in the district. Mrs. Archibald told me at church on Sunday that Dan Trent had hired two women from over Prairie Mound way to cook. She said everyone was raving about the food those women prepared. Now, we can't let the threshers think that the women in this district can't cook as well as they do at Prairie Mound! Thank goodness I have a few tricks up my sleeve yet!" And Mother gave her pie crust a good whack with the rolling pin.

Around eleven o'clock, Mother told Maggie to ride out to the threshers and ask Pa what time the men would be in for dinner. She and Maggie had already put boards in the table so it stretched almost the length of the room, and they had upturned kegs with boards across them for benches since they didn't have enough chairs.

Maggie left Penny firmly tied in her stall, stamping and neighing, but it was Copper's turn for a ride. She pulled him to a halt on a rise and looked in amazement at the busy scene spread before her. The prairies, usually so quiet and calm, were full of noise and action.

The steam engine was roaring and snorting, providing the power through a great revolving belt to the queer-looking separator, which was jiggling and thumping. Two men were throwing wheat sheaves from a huge stack down to two others who were cutting the twine, then throwing the loose sheaves onto the white canvas carrier of the separator. The sheaves were whisked into the machine, and a thick stream of wheat kernels poured out a spout into a sack held by a man who, when it was full, pulled it out of the way and tied it shut. As soon as his sack was full, another man whisked a sack into its place. Straw was tumbling from the carrier and settling in a rising golden mound on the ground.

Maggie saw that Newt Ebenezer and Asa were working together, and she looked for Nicholas. There he was, near Asa, with a pitchfork, struggling to fork the straw away from the engine. Asa was also forking straw, but not so quickly. Newt was shouting something from the seat of a wagon nearly full of sacks bulging with grain. Asa looked up at his father for a minute, then he jabbed Nicholas with his pitchfork, not hard enough to pierce his clothing, but little sharp jabs. Nicholas moved back, but Asa followed, jabbing all the time. Then Maggie saw Pa walk over to the Ebenezers. He and Newt talked a moment, and Pa took Nicholas' pitchfork and threw it up to Newt. Then Pa and Nicholas walked to the water barrel, where the boy began filling stoneware drinking bottles and corking them. Maggie could only guess how much water the men would drink working so hard in the dust and the heat. Nicholas looked up, saw Maggie and gave her a shy little wave, then went back to work with his head down.

Pa told Maggie they would stop for dinner about one o'clock. Maggie galloped back to tell Mother.

Maggie set the table, while Mother mixed a batch of biscuits to put in the oven as soon as the roasts were out. "Some make their biscuits the day before, Ellie, but hot biscuits, fresh from the oven, are something special."

There were three sets of sugars and big white creamers at intervals down the long table, along with pickles, plates of the butter Maggie had churned last week and stacks of homemade bread.

When the men started to file in, after washing their hands at the tin basin set on a stand outside the back door, Mother had the big roasts of beef sliced, and Maggie was putting the vegetable bowls on the table. There were steaming mashed potatoes; thick brown gravy with crackly bits scraped from the roast pan; corn cut from the cobs and cooked in cream, then thickened a bit with flour; mashed turnips; sliced carrots; and a bowl of sauerkraut.

The men came in joking and laughing. Some took off their hats to eat; some didn't. Some had washed their faces as well as their hands; some had eyes showing white in dirty faces. Mr. Phillips-Jones spent some time wetting his hair and combing it just so. Mr. Trent came in late and took just enough time to give his hands a good scrubbing.

Apparently there was only one farm left to thresh after this — Mr. Karlson's. He owned only a quarter section, his original homestead. The men teased him, saying it would take less time to thresh his little fields of grain than to drink a cup of tea, so to make it worth hauling the outfit over there they were going to charge him double. Maggie felt sorry for him because he was so shy that he blushed and couldn't seem to think of a reply. This encouraged the men to tease him even more.

The poor man got a reprieve when they began eating. From the first mouthful they all fell silent and ate as if they must consume everything in sight right now or it might be whisked away and never appear again. Maggie and Mother were kept busy refilling vegetable bowls and pouring strong coffee and tea from blue enamel pots that Mother had steaming on the stove. When the biscuits were cooked and Mother put them on the table with a big jug of golden syrup, a single sigh of satisfaction seemed to come from the men, and Mother almost smiled.

When the plates were empty and the men had wiped them clean with pieces of bread, Mother and Maggie brought out the pies and cakes. There were raisin pies, as well as two kinds of cake. Some men took one sample at a time; others crowded their dinner plates. They poured thick yellow cream over everything before eating.

At the very end of the meal, Mother brought out the special dessert that would keep her reputation as the best cook in the district. She had four pies made from molasses, eggs and cream, flavoured with her secret ingredient, a little vinegar. The men were slowing down, but after they tasted her pie, they dug in and cleaned up every crumb. Mother couldn't hide her pride and satisfaction any longer. She beamed at Maggie over the threshers' heads as she poured more coffee.

When the men went back to the field, Maggie and Mother ate. But they couldn't rest long, because they had to be ready when the men came in for supper. Mother poured hot water from the kettle into the dishpan at one end of the table with a cookie sheet for a draining tray. Mother washed and Maggie dried.

When the dishes were finished and the floor swept, Mother made a huge bread pudding to put in the oven later in the afternoon. Maggie sliced some of the leftover boiled potatoes for frying with onions in big black frying pans. The meat would be served cold tonight, so there was less work than in the morning.

All the extra cooking and washing up took a lot of water. Every few minutes, it seemed, Mother would say, "More water, Ellie. Now don't dawdle!" So Maggie would take the empty water pail to the well, which was nearer the barn than the house, and pump with her aching arms until the pail was full. Then she'd go back to the house, trying to hurry, trying not to spill too much, trying to catch her breath before Mother scolded her for dawdling.

When Miss Fieldmont arrived home after school, she took one look at their tired faces, asked Mother for an apron and pitched in. She helped wait on the men at supper.

When Mr. Trent and Mr. Phillips-Jones came into the kitchen, they looked coldly at each other, then sat as far apart as possible, at opposite ends of a makeshift bench.

Mr. Trent helped himself from the platter of cold meat in front of him. "I hear that those cattle thieves butchered a steer in Archibald's pasture last night. Sure is a mystery."

"I doubt if there's much of a mystery to it!" said Mr. Phillips-Jones, in a tone of voice that suggested he was a little exasperated with Dan Trent for being so dim. "We're only a few hours' ride from Boulder Lake, where all those half-Indians live. I'll wager they're experienced cattle thieves."

There was a moment's silence. Newt Ebenezer nodded. "We're 'most finished the threshing," he said. "In a couple of days we'll have the time to get some men together and go over to Boulder Lake and have a look 'round. What's that big Métis family lives down there? The MacKennas, that's it. There's likely to be somethin' to give them away — steer hide, fresh meat, that sort of thing."

"You'd find the same sort of thing around this farm, Newt," Pa said, his voice tight. "We butchered a heifer last week. You're eatin' it right now. Are you gonna say that the fact we have fresh meat, and there's a fresh hide hangin' in the shed, means I've been stealin' cattle?"

"You make a good point, Trenholme," said Dan Trent. He leaned forward so he could see Mr. Phillips-Jones as he spoke. "Why are you so quick to suspect the Métis, Jones? I've worked with the MacKenna boys ever since I took up my homestead. I figure they're honest men. They're good workers, too."

"Excuse me, my name is Phillips-Jones," protested the handsome man. There were a few grins around the table. Maggie looked quickly at Miss Fieldmont, but couldn't read her expression.

Mr. Phillips-Jones seemed oblivious to the looks. He went on. "I understand these people moved down here from Red River country after the Riel Rebellion. They're not our kind of people. They can't be trusted."

Mr. Trent's voice was low, but so full of emotion it cut through the buzz of conversation around the table. "So, it's length of residency that determines how much someone is to be trusted. Tell me, Jones," and he placed a delicate emphasis on the name, "how long have you lived here?"

"Are you suggesting that you trust ... those people ... before you'd trust me?" Phillips-Jones sputtered.

Pa stood up quickly, knocking his chair backwards as he did so. "Come now! We've got different points of view, but no use gettin' ourselves all worked up. There's threshin' to be done. And I'm ready to get back to it."

Dan Trent hastily drained his cup and followed Pa outside. As the others finished their coffee, they speculated on where the strange cattle thieves would strike next. There seemed to be a pattern. It looked as if the thieves were making a sweep of the district from west to east. So far, all the animals killed had been within half a day's ride of Boulder Lake.

"Didn't I tell you so?" said Phillips-Jones smugly. The men looked at him, then, without speaking, one by one they put on their hats and went back to work.

Miss Fieldmont's face was impossible to read during all this. She insisted on doing the dishes while Mother and Maggie milked the cows. She told them to run along, she needed some time to think.

By the time she fell into bed, Maggie was numb with fatigue. She felt she had just closed her eyes when Mother was shaking her shoulder, saying it would be daylight soon, and they had to get breakfast on.

Mother already had a big pot of porridge bubbling on the back of the stove when Maggie came into the kitchen. The bacon had been sliced the night before and sat in the frying pans; the last of yesterday's boiled potatoes were dotted with butter, in pans to be put in the oven. A basket of eggs stood on the table, waiting to be fried when the crisp bacon was put onto platters in the warming oven.

Maggie set the table, putting big pitchers of milk for the porridge beside the pitchers of cream, and setting out plates of bread and biscuits with blocks of butter and jars of choke-cherry and pincherry jelly. Then she scooped some ground coffee from a paper bag into the blue coffee pots already full of warming water, and set them at the side of the stove to simmer.

Dinner today centred around pork roasts and, for dessert, the special treat was homemade doughnuts and real maple syrup, shipped last spring by relatives in Ontario. Mother said she had hidden a crock away so there'd be some left for harvest time.

The next three days passed in a blur of cooking and cleaning up after meals. Pa came home at dark each night, his face dirty and his step slow with exhaustion, but there was a smile on his face. The wheat was better than anything he'd hoped for and, so far, the weather was holding. Then, on the fourth day, dark clouds were spotted on the horizon in the west, and Pa said that meant rain was coming this way, and gosh-darned but they hadn't finished threshing the oats yet. They needed those oats to feed the animals through the winter, so they had to get them done. And if it rained, he'd be stuck paying the threshers, even when everything had to be shut down, and he wasn't made of money, so they'd all better pray that the rain held off, at least one more day.

The men all cast worried glances toward the horizon. Dan Trent was the first to speak. "There's only three or four hours' more work to finish up here. Why don't we get it over with tonight; then, if it rains tomorrow, we can move the outfit over to Karlson's. And, maybe get a bit of rest until the weather clears."

"That sounds good until you start thinkin'," said Newt Ebenezer. "It's gettin' dark. Don't see how we can work without seein'."

"I think I know how," said Pa. "Look, I've got more straw here than I know what to do with. Let's keep goin' long as we can see anythin', then we can set fire to a straw stack. That'll light things up."

"Sounds like a crazy idea!" said Mother sharply. "There's enough danger of prairie fires in this country without deliberately starting one. We could be burned out, Pa. Just for the sake of saving a few hours."

"There, there, Mother," said Pa. "We're talking about a stack fire, not a prairie fire. We'll plough a firebreak before we start."

Then Pa hitched Belle and Bess up to plough some broad furrows in a big circle around where the men were working. Fire was always dangerous, but now, in the fall, when they hadn't had rain for a while and the stubble fields were dry as old hay, they had to be particularly careful.

So, they finished threshing Pa's oats by the light of a burning straw pile, the flames cracking and roaring, and sparks shooting into the night sky. Mother seemed to be satisfied with the firebreak. "If it wasn't for that fire," she said, "it'd be darker out there than the inside of a cow."

When Maggie awoke in the morning, Mother told her Pa had left a couple of hours ago with Belle and Bess for the Karlson place. The rain seemed to have passed them by to the south, and the men, exhausted as they were, would be threshing again today. Maggie was surprised, then, to see Pa driving up the lane while she was hitching Penny and Copper to the buggy in preparation for going to school. Mother came out on the doorstep, a worried look on her face.

"Whoa, Bess, Belle!" Pa said, then he looked at Maggie and Mother. "That rain we thought passed us by. Well, it was hail. And it didn't pass Karlson's place by. Pounded his stooks into the ground. He can save some for feed maybe, but it's not worth threshin'."

That evening after Maggie went to bed, she could hear Mother and Pa talking about Mr. Karlson as they sat with a cup of tea at the kitchen table. Apparently this was the second year in a row that he had lost his crop. They spoke sorrowfully of his hard work and bad luck. "He's givin' up," said Pa. "Just leavin' everythin' and startin' off in the spring for a new homestead out west. Says this country is against him. Strange idea, but I can understand how he feels."

Maggie felt sad. She sensed that, although Mother and Pa were genuinely sorry for Mr. Karlson, their deepest emotions had been stirred by fear that this land, so bountiful but so unpredictable, might at any moment turn against them and drive them out as well.

To make herself feel better, Maggie thought back to what Mother had told her at breakfast.

"All that wheat! Just think of it. We'll be able to build our new house, *and* pay for your room and board in Valhalla."

Mother's voice had been so hopeful, then. Remembering it, Maggie was able to drift into sleep.

Chapter Sixteen

Our Kind of People

Pa held his hand down to Maggie, caught hers and pulled as she climbed over the wagon wheel, up to the seat beside him. There was a nip in the air, but the sky was blue and the sun scudded in and out among the billowing clouds. High up in the wagon, with Pa whistling beside her and Penny and Copper prancing and dancing down the trail, Maggie was glad to be right here, in Manitoba, and not anywhere else in the whole world.

They were going to Boulder Lake to visit Marie Mac-Kenna, who Pa said ran the biggest farm in the Métis community. Maggie was very excited, because she remembered reading about the Métis. They were descendants of Natives of the western plains, and the first explorers. Many of them still spoke the language of their Aboriginal mothers, but they also spoke French or English of their forefathers. They were a new Canadian people. And Maggie was going to visit one of their homes! Behind her, in the wagon, were some gifts that Mother had sent: a jug of maple syrup and two jars of her pincherry jelly.

After a while, the landscape began to change. There were still grain fields and open prairie around them, but ahead of them was a line of dark wooded hills. Pa had to use the brake on the wagon to keep it from running up against the heels of the team as they descended a winding trail down a hillside. Maggie saw bits of Boulder Lake glimmering through the trees. The air smelled moister here with all the trees around them. It reminded her of New Brunswick.

Maggie heard Marie MacKenna's farmstead before she saw it. There was a yapping of dogs, and shouts floating on the frosty air. As Penny and Copper rounded a bend and trotted into the yard, it seemed that children and dogs ran toward them from every direction.

The yard was full of log buildings, corrals full of horses, a couple of teepees, and, right in the middle of it all, a large log house. It was neatly whitewashed, just like Pa and Mother's house. Pa handed the horses over to a young man, who tied them to a tree. Maggie could see carcasses of game hanging high in the trees, out of reach of the yapping dogs.

Pa and Maggie took Mother's gifts and went to the house. The children swarming around them pushed the door open and ushered them inside. As Maggie's eyes adjusted to the dimness, a woman wearing a long skirt and a green blouse swept down on them. She had bright blue eyes shining from her dark-tanned wrinkled face, and she was smoking a pipe. It was the first time Maggie had seen a woman smoke a pipe, and she realized in a split second that Mother would be cross if she knew she was staring so rudely.

"How are you, Marie? It's been a long time," said Pa, shaking her hand.

"What a bonnie lassie!" the woman said to Maggie, taking her face in her hard wrinkled hands. "That's what my grand-daddy used to say to me." She laughed. "Bet you're surprised. Bet you didn't think I was ever young like you!"

She asked them to sit at the table, while she bustled about filling two bowls from a pot of soup simmering on the stove, and pouring cups of hot, bitter coffee. When Pa gave her Mother's gifts, she thanked him over and over before putting them on a shelf.

As Maggie sipped her soup, she had time to look around. There were dried roots and herbs hanging from the rafters, making the cabin smell wonderful. There were many articles hanging on the walls, some animal hides, some long sashes and broad-brimmed hats, and, on one wall, a fiddle and, beside it, a crucifix.

Eight or nine young men and women came into the room, all wearing a mixture of brightly striped woollen clothing and leather garments. None of them spoke. They leaned against the wall, watching and listening.

"These are some of my sons and their wives," said Marie, waving her arm toward the listeners. "I think you've already met most of my grandchildren."

Pa walked over and shook their hands. He seemed to know a couple of the men. "Harlan, Joe," he said. They ducked their heads to him, smiling shyly.

"This soup sure hits the spot on a cool fall day," said Pa, blowing on a spoonful of the hot liquid before he ate it. "My girl, Ellie, and me came over today to ask you if you'd had any trouble with cattle thieves lately."

Marie sat across the table from them, packing tobacco into the bowl of her pipe. "I heard of them-there thieves," she said, "and my boys have been keeping their eyes open. But, no. We haven't lost a thing. Not so far. You?"

"No," said Pa. "It seems an animal lasts them two or three weeks, then they take another. Appears like it's just a matter of time 'til they get around to us. Glad to hear they haven't come this way. Let us know if anythin' suspicious comes up, Marie. Some of us are thinkin' of callin' in the Mounties."

When Maggie and Pa were ready to drive out of the yard, Marie came running out of the house. Maggie thought she was a very handsome woman, with green ribbons woven into her long dark braids. She reached up and gave Maggie two pairs of moccasins beaded in bright colours. "For you and Mamma," she said.

As they drove out of the yard, children and dogs running after the wagon, Maggie and Pa both turned to wave at Marie standing in the doorway of her cabin.

"That old lady's one of the smartest farmers in this district. Built up a fine herd of horses," said Pa as they drove around the bend in the trail and the farmstead disappeared in the trees behind them. "And she's a good neighbour. She brought over medicine once when I got sick. Must have been an old Cree recipe. Fixed me up right as rain."

He was silent for a moment, and when he spoke his voice was husky. "Can't help thinkin' about what Phillips-Jones said. He's a smart man, educated, from a rich family in the Old Country. The same Old Country your grandpa came from. Said the MacKennas aren't his kind of people. Tell me, Ellie lass, who do you say is our kind of people — Phillips-Jones or the MacKennas?"

Maggie didn't even have to think. "The MacKennas," she said.

"That makes it unanimous," said Pa, laughing and patting her hand. "You and me agree on this one." And Pa whistled the rest of the way home.

Chapter Seventeen

The Home Inspector

When Nicholas brought the cows in for milking one evening, there was a buggy and a single horse in front of the house. The horse was tethered to a block on the ground. Nicholas was letting the cows into the barn when he heard Newt Ebenezer shouting for him to come to the house. Nicholas dropped the milk bucket he was holding and ran.

Inside the house was a strange man. He had sloping shoulders and a big, round stomach. He was dressed in a black suit and wore a necktie. He said to Nicholas that he wanted to go for a little walk.

Nicholas looked at Newt Ebenezer, and was startled because Newt was smiling and nodding. "Go with the gentleman, Nicholas, there's a good lad," he said, his voice unnaturally civil. It was the first time he had ever spoken the boy's name in his presence.

The strange man and Nicholas walked from the house, down the path that led to Matilda Ebenezer's garden. The man said he was a Home Inspector from Winnipeg and he had come to make sure Nicholas was doing well. Then he started asking questions. Was he going to school regularly? How did he like living with the Ebenezers?

Nicholas was careful in his answers. This man was his only hope and he didn't want to say the wrong thing. No, he wasn't going to school. He was kept home to work. Although he worked as hard as he could, he never seemed to please. He admitted he was homesick and missed his mother. He didn't say anything about the beatings and about not getting enough to eat.

He answered truthfully, but the man didn't ask the right questions. After a few moments of silence, the man stopped still. When he turned to Nicholas, his face was dark with anger.

"You ungrateful little wretch! You're nothing but trash from the streets of London, and you come here asking that the world be laid out at your feet. Mr. Ebenezer has been telling me how lazy you are, and how everything's been done for you, but nothing seems to be good enough for Mr. High-and-Mighty English Boy."

He reached out for Nicholas' shoulder as if he meant to give him a good shaking, but Nicholas pulled away. He ran and ran until he reached the willows of the creek and huddled among them, hidden from all eyes.

He knew he would be beaten for running away, but he had to have time to think. He rubbed his eyes on his dirty shirt sleeve and huddled down in his misery.

Maybe it was a few minutes, maybe hours, he was sunk so deeply in despair. But he heard voices. He nestled down closer to the bank of the creek, deep in dried grass, long bare willow branches screening his view. It was Ellie and her mother on the other side of the creek.

Nicholas liked Mrs. Trenholme. When he had been working with the threshing gang, Newt Ebenezer had told him to take some food to the barnyard and eat there, so he would have more time to feed and water the horses. But Mrs. Trenholme had said that, when a boy does a man's work, he must eat like a man. She insisted he sit at the table with the others and made sure he ate until he could hold no more.

Ellie and her mother were on a high place, above the opposite bank. Their voices were low, but they carried clearly on the crisp fall air.

"I haven't had time to come down here for weeks," said Mrs. Trenholme. "Look how it's overgrown with grass! It's a scandal!" As she spoke, she was cutting grass with a small scythe. Then she threw down the scythe and began to pull grass with her hands. Appearing from the mass of tangled growth was a wooden cross. "There now, Ellie. There's the balsams I planted on the grave. If we had the time, it would never get overgrown like this, but somehow I think your grandfather would understand."

Her voice rose and fell with the rhythm of her work, but Nicholas could hear every word. "You were too young when he died, Ellie, to remember much about him. He liked growing things. Most farmers think only of growing their crops, but your grandfather was different. He liked to grow flowers and cabbages and all sorts of things that you can't rightly say are things you farm."

Ellie was working all this time, pulling grasses and digging out roots of weeds. Sometimes she stopped for a moment, as if she wanted to speak, but her mother didn't pause in her story. "When he got old and knew he didn't have long, he asked to be buried by the creek because he loved it so. At first your pa said no, the water would rise and wash out the grave. But your grandpa knew this high spot that the water never gets to. And he knew there's a blanket of crocuses along here in spring, and wild roses and tiger lilies in summer. And down there, in the moist flats, there's ladies' slippers. Ah, he loved Manitoba, Ellie."

Mrs. Trenholme straightened up and rubbed her back. "He wasn't well when we came out here and left all our people back in Ontario, but he was even more excited than your pa. He called this God's country. He said Manitoba was for new starts, and coming here gave him another go at life. He walked all the way out here from Winnipeg behind the oxen. You were a baby, so I rode some, but that old man walked every step of the way."

Mrs. Trenholme bent over and went back to weeding while she kept up her stream of talk. "Even those first two years of homesteading, with all the work and heartbreak, he never complained. And when he got too poorly to help Pa in the fields, he helped me in the house. And how he loved you, child. I always scolded that he was spoiling you, but he could never see it that way."

Nicholas could see Ellie clearly. She seemed to be listening intently to her mother.

Mrs. Trenholme smoothed her hands against her skirts and said for Ellie not to take too long finishing up, because she needed the wood box filled before supper. Then she hurried away.

Nicholas waited in his hiding place for a few minutes. In another minute, he had crossed the shallow creek by balancing on a row of stones he and Ellie had built a fording place with. Ellie was subdued, still working at her grandfather's gravesite. Nicholas read the words carved into the cross: "Timothy Blaire Trenholme, 1802-1882, Gone Home."

"Gone home," Nicholas repeated slowly. "He was lucky."

Ellie turned to him at the sound of his wistful voice. "What's the matter, Nicholas?"

He was grateful for her presence. He had to talk to someone or burst. He told her about the Home Inspector. Ellie seemed as disheartened as he was; they had both talked so often about how things would improve when the inspector came.

Ellie was looking at him strangely. "I just thought of a way you can get away from the Ebenezers and have a better life," she said. She took him by the hand and led him to a place where they could sit and watch the sun set, and she began talking quietly, gazing at the western sky as she spoke.

Her story was stranger than any he could imagine. She wasn't who everyone thought she was. She wasn't Ellie at all. Her name was Maggie, she was from another century, and she had travelled back in time. This was the second such journey she had made. She didn't have any control over this travelling, but she knew, she was sure, that when the time was right the waterfall would appear again and take her home.

"I want you to come with me, Nicholas," she said, looking directly into his eyes. "You can live with us. Aunt Kate and Uncle Jeff and I all live in a very big house. There's more than enough room. You don't need to go outdoors to the bathroom and you can fill the tub with hot water just by turning a tap. There is a nice school, and buildings are warm, and you can get all the sleep you need and ... oh, Nicholas, I really want you to come!"

He couldn't take all this in for a moment. Ellie's offer sounded exciting and tempting. The life she described sounded unimaginably easy. It lured him the way a golden palace in a magic land did when his mother told him fairy tales. Suddenly he realized just what Ellie had been saying to him. A fairy tale! He was suddenly angry with her, so angry he was shaking.

"You're making fun of me," he shouted. "I trusted you. I thought I could tell you everything. Then you give me this far-fetched tale! You must think I'm witless — that I'd believe such nonsense!"

Maggie stared at him with such genuine consternation that his anger died. He stood there, confused.

Maggie's forehead was creased with concentration. Suddenly she grinned and grabbed his arm. "Come with me, Nicholas. I can prove that I come from the future!"

She hustled him across the pasture to the Trenholmes' house. Inside, the kitchen was empty. She called her mother's name and, when there was no answer, she pulled Nicholas into the lean-to shed. There, she opened a rough wood box.

"Your father was a bootmaker, right?"

"Master bootmaker," Nicholas answered, puzzled at her question.

"And you were learning to be a bootmaker at the orphanage, right?"

"All the boys were taught a trade. I wasn't there long, but one day I'll be a bootmaker like me dad. I will. You'll see," he said in a determined voice, although he couldn't really believe anymore, since the visit of the Home Inspector, that any of his dreams would ever come true.

While they were talking, Maggie was rummaging in the box. She took out layers of folded clothes and laid them on the floor. Finally, she found what she was looking for. She pulled from the bottom of the box the strangest-looking boots that Nicholas had ever seen.

He took one from her outstretched hand and examined it carefully. It was made of scuffed white leather. It was low cut, and inside there were layers of a flexible material he had never seen before. The sole was the strangest of all. It was a thick, dirty-white, spongy, yet hard stuff, with grooves cut through it.

"I don't see how the bootmaker made this," he said. "Where's the stitching?"

"It wasn't handmade," said Maggie. "It's called a sneaker and it was made in a factory along with thousands and thousands of others just like it. It's from the next century, Nicholas. In my time, this is the kind of shoes most kids, I mean children, wear."

She looked so sincere. Nicholas stared at her a moment, then back at the strange boot. He didn't know what to think. He said nothing. Then Maggie went to her bed and pulled some things out from under the mattress. She held up a white shirt with no buttons and some trousers.

"These are the clothes I was wearing when I came here in the waterfall," she said. She was looking at him closely. "You believe me now, don't you?"

Nicholas looked once more at the strange boot. He couldn't imagine another explanation for it. He nodded his head, slowly.

"Great!" she said. "Then you'll come back with me to my time? All your troubles will be over."

Nicholas handed her back her sneaker and there was a long moment of silence before he spoke. Then he dropped his eyes from her hopeful, excited face. "I couldn't leave me mum behind," he said, quietly.

Maggie swallowed hard. Tears welled up in her eyes.

As they faced each other, neither speaking, Maggie wiped her cheeks with the back of her hand. Nicholas felt something shifting inside him. He realized now that this girl, Maggie she called herself, had come on a much longer journey than he had. He was shaken by the wonder of her story. He was overwhelmed with her courage.

All these weeks, since he'd come to Manitoba, he'd been putting up with injustice, waiting for someone else to fix things. Since the visit from the Home Inspector, he knew that wasn't going to happen. What could he do now? Of one thing he was sure. He wasn't going to let the Ebenezers bully him for three more years.

"I've got to do it myself," he blurted.

"Do what?" she asked.

"Find a way to get away from the Ebenezers and make my way in the world so I can bring Mum over."

"But, how?" asked Maggie.

"I don't know, yet. But I'll find a way." His voice sounded more sure than he felt. His stomach was clenching, for even as he spoke he remembered the words of the Home Inspector, that he was nothing but trash. Those words had hurt him as much as Newt Ebenezer's thrashings.

"Can I help?" asked Maggie.

"I don't mind taking help," said Nicholas. "But I don't even know what kind of help I need. I only know I can't go in your waterfall with you. I've got to fight me own battles."

He thought a minute, then looked at her shyly. "Do you think I could ride your horses sometime?"

Maggie looked astonished. "I've offered them to you, over and over. I thought you didn't like ... When would you ever ... ?"

"There are some things I've got to do," he said simply.

"I can tether the horses in the pasture at night," Maggie said, quietly. "Pa said it would be all right until the snow comes. To let them graze as much as possible."

"Thanks," Nicholas said. He had never told Maggie how terrified he was of horses. It was something so deep in his very being that he couldn't find the words.

Chapter Eighteen

A Letter to London

Pa said he was going to town. He would be going to the boot-and-harness shop to do some business. He knew Ellie would come, but did Mother want to come? Or Miss Fieldmont?

Mother said she wouldn't go today. She had a bad cold, so she was heating some goose grease for her chest, and would stay warm at home with a cup of ginger tea at her side while she caught up on some mending.

Miss Fieldmont also elected to stay home. She had bought a length of soft brown wool and was struggling to make a dress. Mother offered to help her.

"Isn't it strange that there isn't a dressmaker in a town as big as Valhalla," said Miss Fieldmont. "If there were one, I'd certainly make use of her services." She sighed and sucked a finger she'd just pricked with a pin.

Maggie's head snapped up. A dressmaker in Valhalla! She knew that Nicholas' mother was a dressmaker, for Nicholas talked about her all the time. Why not bring his mother to Manitoba to work? She remembered the empty rooms over Kristjana's father's shop. It would be a perfect place for a dressmaker's business.

"Pa," she said, "could we take Nicholas Camper with us to town? There's lots of room in the buggy and I don't think he's ever been there." She was clasping her hands in front of her and rising up and down on her toes as she spoke.

Pa looked doubtful. "I don't think Newt Ebenezer would want the boy to take time off from work," he said.

"The point should be," said Mother, "whether the boy should have some time off — not what Newt Ebenezer says. The last time I looked, he wasn't the prime minister or a police chief. Just a mean old skinflint that makes his family miserable."

Mother turned to Miss Fieldmont to explain. "I went to school with poor Matilda Ebenezer back in Ontario before she married Newt. She was the prettiest girl in our school. She was courted by a fine young man, Jimmy Bayers. If she'd married him, she wouldn't have the worries she has today. But, as I always say, you can go through the woods and go through the woods and pick up a crooked stick at last."

"I think you're right, Mrs. Trenholme," said Miss Fieldmont. "The boy should have an outing. And he should be coming to school!"

Pa's face was screwed up, which showed he was thinking. Finally he spoke. "I'm goin' over there and take that lad to town. Why, I'll bet he's never had a treat since he came here. Come on, Ellie, we'd better get goin' or we won't get back before nightfall."

It was two determined people who drove into the Ebenezers' yard. Maggie was shocked at the state of the place. Broken farm implements and parts of machines were scattered here and there over the sparse dry grass. A huge teepee-shaped pile of poplar logs was standing near the house. Nicholas had a log across a stump and was sawing off stove lengths. A haphazard pile of sticks was growing beside him as he worked. There were no flowers near the house, no little trees like the ones Mother had planted with seeds she had brought from Ontario. A washtub, a washboard and a scrub pail and mop lay in the dust outside the door.

Inside, the house was no better. The earthen floor was spattered with spilled food, and smoke was pouring from every crack in the old stove. Matilda Ebenezer moved slowly and heavily. Maggie hadn't known she was expecting a baby. No one talked about such things here, but it looked as if the baby would be coming very soon.

The poor woman seemed shy and flustered. But she had manners. She asked them to sit and offered a cup of tea. They refused politely, saying they were on their way to town and had stopped to offer Nicholas a ride.

Pa asked if Newt was home, so Matilda Ebenezer sent Cora running to the barn to find him. Asa came into the kitchen and quietly sat at the kitchen table. Maggie thought he looked kind of pitiful. He didn't act with so much bravado when he didn't have the other big boys to impress.

Newt came into the house, full of smiles. What a hypocrite, thought Maggie. He shook Pa's hand, but only mumbled a curt hello to Maggie. Maggie was horrified when he spit a stream of tobacco juice into the pigs' pail of potato peelings and food scraps that stood by the door. Maggie noticed that Asa stiffened when his father appeared, and he got that cruel look on his face that she hated so much.

"Newt, we've come about the English boy," said Pa, never one to beat around the bush.

Newt Ebenezer's smile faded. "Now, Trenholme," he said, "I never thought you'd be the type to meddle in other people's business."

"As a rule, I'm not," said Pa. "But in a way this is my business. I'm on the school board, Newt. We came to take the boy to town. For an outin'. Let him come for the afternoon, We'll have him back by milkin' time. We'll talk more about this school thing later."

"No!" Newt Ebenezer snarled. "This here boy is meant to work and I've got the signed papers to prove it. A contract between me and that there orphanage. He's legally bound to work for me 'til he's sixteen, not to go gallivantin' 'round the country. He nearly eats me out of house and home, and you want him to miss a whole afternoon's work. For the last time, he's not goin' to school, and he's not goin' to town!"

"Yes, I am," said a voice from the doorway. They all turned to see Nicholas standing there with an armload of wood.

Nicholas had been standing there long enough to hear Newt Ebenezer's words. One part of his mind was pleased that Mr. Trenholme cared about him. But, even so, Newt Ebenezer's cruel words seemed to ignite something deep in him which had been smouldering ever since the Home Inspector had turned on him.

"Thank you for the offer, Mr. Trenholme," he heard himself say in a firm, strong voice. "I've wanted to see Valhalla ever since I came on the train. I didn't get a chance to see much that day. I'll just go up and change my clothes. I'll be ready in a tick."

If a bomb had gone off, the adults in the room wouldn't have been more astonished. Newt Ebenezer's mouth hung open. Matilda Ebenezer looked as if she might cry. She kept staring at her husband, but of course he couldn't do anything in front of their neighbours. Asa seemed the most astonished of all. As if mesmerized, he sat with his eyes fixed on the trapdoor in the ceiling through which Nicholas had disappeared.

Newt Ebenezer rose from his chair and began pacing. Suddenly he turned on Cora and shouted for her to get out to the garden and get back to work. Cora scampered away, obviously frightened.

"I'll go and help her," said Asa defiantly. He stood up so fast his chair toppled over. Newt stared after him, so amazed at this second act of defiance in one afternoon that he forgot to spit his tobacco juice and swallowed a mouthful, a look of sick horror crossing his face as he did so.

Nicholas hurried to change from his dirty, torn overalls into his wool suit with the short pants. They were tight on him now. And the pants were shorter than ever. He hadn't realized until now how much he had grown, although he had known for some time that his feet were growing because his boots had become so tight he now usually went barefoot.

When he came down, Newt had gone back to the barn, and Mrs. Ebenezer gave him a wavering smile but didn't speak. Mr. Trenholme and Maggie were waiting in the buggy. Asa stood by the house, staring at him with a look of deep concentration. Penny and Copper, sensing the tension in the air, took off at a quick trot, the buggy wheels bouncing over frozen ruts in the trail, making Nicholas hang on. He caught Maggie's eye and they grinned at each other. But even as he grinned, Nicholas was thinking about what would happen when he came home.

In town, they drove to the boot-and-harness shop. Mr. Jonsson was busy resoling some boots. He barely looked up, but seemed happy to talk as he worked. Pa told Maggie to skedaddle while he did his business. For some reason, he said he didn't mind if Nicholas stayed.

Maggie ran upstairs. In a minute she came back with a pretty girl with freckles on her nose. They said they were going to Kwan's for ice cream and asked Nicholas to go with them, but he said no thank you. He didn't have any money, and the second, more powerful, reason he refused was that he wanted to spend every minute he could right here in the shop.

After the girls left, Mr. Trenholme was deep in conversation with Mr. Jonsson, so Nicholas had time to look around. The smell of leather brought back a rush of memories of his father's shop. He felt like burying his face in the long, smooth sheets of tanned leather, but he contented himself with running his fingers over smooth and rough pieces, and realized he was sensing the quality of each.

There was a long workbench near the front, near big windows that let in the light. The workbench was made of a thick plank set on posts, something so sturdy and heavy that it seemed to have grown there, right where it stood, and would remain there always. There were nicks and gouges in its dark surface, and a vice was attached at one end.

The bench was cluttered with shoe lasts, open containers of nails and rivets, hammers of different sizes and cutting shears, all implements he'd been familiar with in his father's shop. There were shelves along one wall filled with boots, some newly made, some waiting for repair. Hanging on the opposite wall and across the back of the shop were sets of harness, and saddles. There was a whole row of bridles decorated with brasses. They were *beautiful*, he thought, *smashing*. He'd never seen anything like them in his life, and scattered across the floor were boxes, some with boots or harness waiting for mending. Thrown in piles, here and there, were scraps of leather.

Mr. Jonsson finished the resoling job, attached a scrap of paper with the owner's name on it, then put the boots up on a shelf. He immediately went back to work on a pair of boots he said had been ordered by the doctor's wife. He had a piece of

130

cardboard with the outline of her feet. "I always get an outline of both feet for an order, he said, because —"

"Because most people have feet that are slightly different in size, and sometimes in shape," finished Nicholas.

"Not many people know that," said Mr. Jonsson, looking over his glasses. "Especially young men. Tell me, Nicholas, where did you learn such a thing?"

"I remember hearing me dad say that. He was a master bootmaker in London. But he's dead now," Nicholas said simply. "When I was little, I used to help in the shop. Would you mind very much if I sorted those piles of leather scraps on the floor over there? I could put them in boxes according to their size — or the weight of the leather — or whatever you'd like." He finished a little lamely, afraid that Mr. Jonsson might think he was too forward.

But the man just laughed. "It's not often someone comes in and offers to help. I'd be a fool to say no. You can see I don't have time to keep things neat and clean."

By mid-afternoon, when Mr. Trenholme had finished his other business in town and come back for Nicholas, the boy had sorted the leather scraps, swept the floor and begun the huge task of organizing rivets and nails according to size. He was reluctant to leave, but Mr. Trenholme said that Penny and Copper were pawing the ground, they were so anxious to head home. So Nicholas took one last lungful of leather-perfumed air and left.

Maggie prattled on as the horses trotted down the street. She was full of excitement about what Kristjana had been telling her about town. "She loves books as much as I do. And she says she'll be old enough to join the Literary Society soon. That's just a bunch of people who get together and talk about books. There are all sorts of things to do in town. She even plays tennis." She spoke as if all this was too much to believe.

"But she's very jealous of me having two riding horses. Can I invite her to the farm so I can teach her to ride, Pa?"

"You'll have to ask Mother," said Pa, "but, just between you and me, I'd guess she'd say yes. The Jonssons are good people. I think she'd approve."

Then he turned to Nicholas. "Tell Ellie what Fridbjorn said to you," he said.

"Oh, Ellie," said Nicholas, "I forgot you didn't know already! He asked me to be his apprentice. He said he needs help ever so much and I could live there and help him and learn the trade and go to school."

"Nicholas!" Maggie said, emotion turning her voice to a whisper.

"But, I'm legally bound to stay with the Ebenezers until I'm sixteen. Unless my mother comes to claim me. That's the only way I'd be free. So, we've just got to get my mother over here."

"*Just,*" said Maggie. "That sounds like a big just."

"Mr. Jonsson wrote to Miss Charity at the Lost Lambs Orphanage. He told her there are rooms in his building where Mum could set up a dressmaking shop. She'll put Mum on a ship, and when she gets here, we ..." Nicholas' voice drifted away, suddenly overcome with his feelings.

They pulled up to the hitching rail in front of the post office while Nicholas ran in and mailed the letter that Mr. Jonsson had written to Miss Charity. When he climbed into the buggy, he asked Mr. Trenholme how long it would take for a letter to get all the way to London.

"Seems to me a few weeks. First the train all the way east, then a ship across the ocean. Then this here Miss Charity has to answer, and her letter will take some weeks to get back. We'll be lucky to hear by Christmas, son. And don't be surprised if we don't hear until later than that."

Nicholas and Maggie looked at each other. They both felt a little deflated, realizing this would take much longer than they'd first thought.

"It won't seem so long," said Maggie, in a forced cheerful way.

"No, not long at all," said Nicholas, his voice small and tired.

That night, when the house was quiet, Nicholas crept silently down the ladder from his loft and went outside. A giant moon hung in the sky. Mr. Trenholme had called it a harvest moon.

Every bone in his body was aching. He had welts on the backs of his legs from the willow switch Newt had whipped him with when he got back from Valhalla. But, as he hurried across the pasture in the moonlight, the pain was pushed out of his mind by thoughts of horses, and his fear.

He had been coming to where Penny and Copper were tethered every night since that day he'd decided he had to take his fate in his own hands. When everyone else was sleeping, he had patted the horses and talked to them. They recognized him now, and whickered when he appeared. They seemed less like dangerous beasts and more like welcoming friends on each visit. On the last few nights he had screwed up his courage and mounted one, then the other, but he had not untied the ropes that tethered them. He had just sat on their backs, feeling their warmth through his work pants, getting a little giddy each time they moved.

Tonight, he decided, had to be the night. If he was going to make his way in this country, he had to learn to ride. Horses were everywhere, in town as well as the country. When Maggie talked about Bess and Belle, Penny and Copper, she spoke as if they were members of the family. Like people, they had their own personalities.

He knew Penny was Maggie's favourite, but he liked Copper best. When Maggie rode Copper across the pasture, his four white feet flashing, he looked as if he was flying above the ground.

Nicholas' hand was trembling as he untied the halter rope, and he realized that he was the only thing between the horse and freedom. Copper shook his head up and down and snorted. Nicholas tightened his grip on the rope. Then he grasped Copper's mane and jumped to his back. It was a trick he had been practising for several nights, and he felt proud that he no longer needed to climb on something in order to mount the horse.

He pulled the rope to the right and urged the animal forward by clicking his tongue, as he had heard Maggie do. Copper started to trot, his head high, his neck arched.

"Whoa," Nicholas yelled, nearly frantic with fear, and the horse stopped still. The movement was so abrupt that Nicholas was thrown forward, against the gelding's neck. He felt himself sliding to the ground. His muscles were rigid with effort, but he couldn't catch himself and he bumped to the earth at Copper's feet. The gelding swung his head and nosed him curiously. Nicholas picked himself up quickly and dusted himself off. The fall had inflamed the pain in his bruised legs and back. His breath was coming in ragged gasps, as if he had run a long race. His heart was beating fast, but he was determined.

Before he had time to think, he was up on Copper, riding again. Within half an hour, he had fallen four times, but each time he quickly remounted. Nicholas was learning more each time about letting his body follow the rhythm of the horse, but, even more important, he was discovering that the voice signals Maggie had taught him — whoa, git up, haw, gee, easy now — got an instant response from Copper.

By the time he had retethered Copper next to Penny, forded the creek and limped painfully back to the Ebenezers' homestead, the moon was low in the sky. His exhaustion was so overwhelming, he had to concentrate to put one foot in front of another. He knew he was close to being able to ride, after a fashion, but he still had so much to learn. Would he have the strength to keep coming out at night until he had mastered it? Right now, he didn't think so.

But, when he at last climbed the creaking ladder and fell into an exhausted sleep, for the first time since he had come to Canada he had pleasant dreams. He dreamt of the smell of wild sage and grasses, warm in the sun. And, in his dream, he and a girl with long hair were riding winged horses, flying fearlessly and powerfully high above the wide prairies.

When he was shaken awake in the morning, he could barely move his stiff, sore body. Then he remembered his dream and he smiled. Just the thought of riding a flying horse filled him with strength and hope.

Chapter Nineteen

Prairie Fire

Mother and Maggie did the milking morning and night when Pa was busy in the fields working long days, doing his fall work. Maggie liked barn work, but it was more fun when Pa was cheerfully whistling in the next stall or telling funny stories. Mother always seemed afraid that the horses would step on Maggie's foot, or the cows would kick her, or she'd step on a pitchfork, or she'd fall prey to dozens of other dangers. Maggie tried to ignore the scolding, warning voice, but it was impossible.

After they finished milking, Mother set aside the pails of milk in the sod shanty, where it was cool. She would leave the milk there until the cream rose to the top, then she would skim the cream off and pour it into a can with a tight-fitting lid. Because the can was heavy, Maggie had to help hold the rope as they slowly lowered it into the well. The rope burned Maggie's hands as she tried to keep it from slipping too fast, until the can was suspended far down. Way down there, where the water glistened in the dimness, the cold well water would keep the cream cool and sweet. Mother warned her every day not to lean too far forward lest she fall in and drown.

Maggie was fascinated by the shanty where the milk was left to cool. She knew the story of it, because she had asked Pa so many questions about it.

When Pa and Mother came to homestead in Manitoba, they bought a team of oxen to haul their belongings from Winnipeg out to their homestead. It was spring time and they had to hurry to break a bit of the land, get a crop in, and plant a garden to feed themselves. They had no time to build a proper house, so they lived in a tent at first. In the fall the nights started getting cool and they knew they had to have somewhere better before winter came, so Pa used the oxen to haul sods. The neighbours came over to help, and in a few days they had built a small house, with the sods used like bricks in the walls. For a roof they laid a framework of poplar poles and covered them with sods. So the roof had grass growing on it. They had created something like a cave.

Pa and Mother lived in the shanty for two years, until they had enough money to build the house they were in now.

"It was awful," Mother said when Maggie asked her about it. "I felt like a gopher living in a hole, it was so dark, with dirt walls and a dirt floor. Just like a little gopher hole. Our mattress was on some planks Pa put across one end of the room, and that took a third of the space. Your grandfather had a pallet he slept on that he rolled up every morning. We could sit at the table and take the food off the stove without getting up, it was so cramped. And when it rained, the sods on the roof would get soaked through and the water would drip, drip, drip for two or three days after the rain stopped. I had to set cans everywhere to catch the water. You were so small — I was always afraid you'd catch pneumonia — and us out here so far from a doctor."

"Now, now," Pa said when he heard Mother. "You worried for nothing. Ellie's never been sick a day in her life. Living in the soddie wasn't so bad, as I see it. We were never cold in it. The wind didn't blow in all the cracks like it does here in the house."

Maggie liked skimming the milk in the sod house. Even in the heat of the day it was cool and moist, and it smelled of earth and growing things. It was mysterious in the dimness. She heard rustlings in the corners. She knew it was just mice looking for a sheltered place to spend the winter, but she liked to pretend it was voices whispering, telling secrets.

Pa hauled one load of wheat to Valhalla to sell. Maggie rode with him, high up on the wagon seat. Belle and Bess pulled the wagon loaded high with sacks of wheat, their muscles rippling under their shiny coats. At the elevator, Pa dumped the wheat out of the sacks into a barred opening in the floor. The elevator man weighed it and tested it. The wheat would be shipped out on the train, Pa told Maggie, and, in a few weeks, they would get a cheque in the mail from Winnipeg.

Pa was always whistling these days. He bought Maggie a bag of candies when she went with him to town, but warned her not to let Mother know. Mother didn't think treats were good for young people. "Those who get things handed to them never learns to get," she would tell Pa whenever he bought something for Maggie.

But, Mother wasn't grumbling so much these days. She was planning the new house. It was going to be built of lumber, not logs. It would have an upstairs with three bedrooms and a big kitchen, a back kitchen and a parlour.

"No use having a parlour," said Pa, "when we don't have a blessed stick of furniture to put in it."

Then Mother got out the Eaton's catalogue and showed him a sideboard she had her eye on. It had a high, elaborately carved back with a mirror in the centre. "Now, don't say we can't afford it, Pa, with all that wheat out in the bin. I figure, if we have more crops like this, we can buy a new piece of furniture every year, until we have a parlour as fine as any in town!"

Then Mother flipped the pages of the catalogue until she came to the pianos and the organs. Pa went back to the barn, whistling all the way.

Pa was breaking some new land these cool fall days. He hitched Belle and Bess to the breaking plough each morning, and all three came home at night so tired their heads hung low. So, he put off hauling the rest of the grain to town until winter. Except for a few mice nibbling at it, it was out of harm's way in the bin on the far side of the barnyard.

One Saturday, Miss Fieldmont went out riding with Mr. Trent on his beautiful black riding horses. She had been invited by the minister's wife to spend the night in town, and he was going along to make sure she got there safely.

Mother's rare smile lit up her face. She didn't tell Miss Fieldmont how much the family was hoping she would choose Mr. Trent.

Two of her hens were so old they weren't producing enough eggs to bother with, so Mother took the hatchet, chopped off their heads and asked Maggie to help her get the birds ready for stewing for Sunday dinner.

Maggie had her sleeves rolled up and was cleaning the hens when she heard the thunder. The sky got dark, but there was no rain, only peals of thunder and flashes of lightning. As Maggie finished, Mother began cutting the hens into pieces and put them into a kettle with some chopped onions.

"I can manage this, Ellie," she said. "Why don't you run to the barn and help your pa. He can't do everything by himself, you know."

Pa was standing in front of the barn, looking westward. When Maggie ran up, he didn't look at her, but continued to stare into the distance. There, far on the horizon, she saw what he was looking at. At first she thought it was clouds of dust, billowing dark so far away.

"Smoke," said Pa. "With all the rain we had in the summer, the grass is thicker than mosquitoes at a picnic. Now, we haven't had rain in weeks and the prairie's dry as tinder. Just right for a grand-daddy of a prairie fire. I fear the lightnin's gone and set it off." His voice sounded tired. He licked his finger and held it up. "Wind's from the south. Lucky it's not from the west, or it'd blow the fire our way."

In a few moments, Mother joined them, standing by Pa and frowning as they watched the smoke rolling across the plains.

"Good thing I just did that breakin' north of the house," said Pa. "I'll work on a firebreak to the west. That's where it's comin' from — now. Won't have time to do anythin' on the south. Just have to trust our luck."

"Will the fire come here?" asked Maggie, beginning to get scared.

"Maybe. It can turn if it hits water. Or a wide-enough firebreak. If the wind changes it can turn in the twinklin' of an eye. We have some time to get ready. It's a long ways away."

Pa got the tired team and drove them out beyond the farmyard and began to plough a firebreak.

The family slept uneasily that night, a faint smell of smoke invading their dreams. By morning, the wind had changed to the west, and Pa became very worried. He looked at the strip of firebreak ploughed in the black earth west of the barn and decided it wasn't enough. He and Mother went beyond it and set fire to the grass. When Maggie asked what they were doing, they said they were burning a bare patch, so the fire would have nothing to feed on if it came this way. When Maggie begged to help, Mother told her to stay away from the burning: it was too dangerous.

Pa told Maggie she could help by letting the animals out of the barn. If the fire jumped the firebreak, he didn't want them tied in their stalls, unable to escape.

When Mother and Pa came into the house for dinner, their faces were black with smoke and their eyes were red-rimmed with fatigue and fear. Maggie put cold meat and pickles and bread on the table, and they ate without speaking.

After their hasty meal, Pa and Mother carried armloads of grain sacks to the well, laid them in the horse trough and told Maggie to pump water on them until they were soaked through. Then they went for more.

They could see the fire now, low red lines of flame snaking along the ground, with clouds of smoke above it. They could hear the hissing and crackling. Then Pa shouted, "Look! Look at the wild things!"

There, running ahead of the flames, were dozens of little animals: rabbits, foxes, gophers, prairie chickens, things Maggie couldn't name. She had never seen anything so terrifying as all those innocent creatures racing from the flames.

Then, the line of animals, as one, veered to the south and raced in a crowd across the pasture.

"Instinct,' said Pa. "Somethin' tells them to go to the creek. The water's low, but it'll probably be enough to save them. If it was any higher, we'd go there ourselves."

The fire was in a long line to the west, still racing in their direction. As it got closer, the crackling and snapping got louder and the smoke thicker.

"Oh," said Mother, and her voice was almost a wail, "I don't think the firebreak can hold it."

"Quick, to the soddie," said Pa. "It won't burn!"

They huddled inside. It was cool there, in the old sod house. Outside the air was hot and dry, but inside there was still the damp smell of fresh earth. They were too tired, too terrified to talk. There were no openings on the west side of the soddie, so they couldn't see the fire. Gradually the air in the little house began to smell of smoke.

They could see their house through a hole in the wall. They could see the pasture through the open door. Smoke swirled in the air, and sparks and burning flakes fell about and fizzled out on the ground.

"Look," shouted Pa.

The pasture was on fire. But the fire was moving south, toward the creek.

"Thank God!" said Mother. "The wind must have changed."

They waited a few moments, watching the fire roar through the thick dried grass of the pasture, gripping one another's hands.

Then they went outside. Mother looked around the yard and shouted, "The grain bin. It's on fire!"

Pa ran for the wheelbarrow, then Mother and Maggie helped him pile the wet sacks high on it and they raced to the bin. Pa climbed on the roof, and Maggie halfway up the ladder to hand him the sacks that Mother was passing to her. Mother was so beside herself that, for once, she didn't caution Maggie about the danger of climbing ladders.

Pa beat at the flames with the wet sacks. They seemed to die down for a moment, then spring up somewhere else. It wasn't until the heat and the smoke drove them away that they knew they had lost the fight.

The three of them stood helplessly, their lips and throats parched and aching, their eyes squinting through the smoke, their skin hot and scorched, and watched the flames leap higher and higher as smoke from all those sacks of burning grain billowed into the prairie sky.

Pa stood between Mother and Maggie. "At least you're both safe," he said. "And all the stock. We should be thankful."

"Miss Fieldmont and Mr. Trent?" asked Maggie in a croak, suddenly thinking of the danger to their friends.

"I don't think the fire would come anywhere near Valhalla," Pa said. "They'll be safe."

Mother was crying soundlessly, her shoulders shaking.

Exhausted, they dragged themselves back to the house. Pa spoke again of how lucky they were to still have a house.

They were parched. They took turns drinking from the dipper in the water pail until they had used up all the fresh water. Then Mother went into her bedroom and shut the door. She still hadn't spoken.

"Wash up and go to bed, lassie," said Pa, his voice husky. "Tomorrow we'll find out how the neighbours made out." Then he went into the bedroom, and Maggie heard him say, "There, there, lass. Don't you go on, now. What's a little wheat, anyway? We'll plant more next year."

There was a pause, and when he spoke again his voice was stronger. "Whatever else you say about this country, there's always next year!"

Chapter Twenty

The Bill Bristol Gang

The people of the district considered themselves lucky. A lot of prairie land had been burned over, but no one was hurt and only one house had been lost. The fire had jumped the creek on Mr. Trent's place and burned his house to the ground. Luckily, he had already hauled his harvest to the elevator, so he'd have money to build again.

The excitement over the prairie fire had barely died down when the cattle thieves struck, closer to home this time. They butchered a heifer in Newt Ebenezer's pasture.

Friday afternoon, Pa came home from Valhalla with the mail and the latest news. The whole town was in an uproar of excitement. Newt Ebenezer and Mr. Phillips-Jones had met the train on Friday, picked up a Mountie and drove him out to the MacKennas' farm. The Mountie had found evidence of freshly killed beef. He had arrested two of the MacKenna boys, brought them into town and put them in the lock-up.

144

"Now they're a couple of accused criminals waiting for the magistrate to come so's they can have a trial," Pa explained to Maggie and Miss Fieldmont. He was furious. "I've known Joe and Harlan MacKenna for years. They're no more cattle thieves than I am. But some likes to think the worst of other folks."

"It's the first time anyone's ever been arrested since the lock-up was built five years ago," said Mother. "That's why everyone's so excited."

The next morning, Mother and Pa decided to go to Valhalla for the day. There was going to be a ball game in the afternoon and the Methodist church was having its yearly bazaar. Mother said she might buy a few things, if they were reasonable, and put them away for Christmas. Pa said he'd like to see how Fridbjorn was doing on a little something he was working on. Miss Fieldmont said she'd like to visit her friend, the minister's wife, and maybe help at the bazaar.

Maggie begged to be allowed to stay home. Mother fussed but Pa was on Maggie's side. Maggie told him she wanted to go for a horseback ride, and he said he thought they could manage by taking the work team to town and leaving Penny and Copper with her. Then Maggie told Mother that she had a lot of Latin verbs to study, and Miss Fieldmont nodded her head, so Mother finally said yes, as long as she promised that she wouldn't try anything dangerous when she was on her own.

As soon as Belle and Bess trotted out of the yard, Maggie ran to the barn and bridled Penny. She made sure Copper was firmly tied to his manger, and took off across the prairie, toward Boulder Lake.

Maggie was as upset as Pa was that the MacKennas were accused of stealing. She hoped that she might be able to help them. Maybe Mrs. MacKenna had some theories about the thefts and Maggie could pass on the information.

She rode to the MacKennas' homestead. It took less time to get there today because, on horseback, Maggie could cut across the prairie instead of going around by the road, as she and Pa had done with the wagon.

Marie MacKenna shuffled toward Maggie like an old, old woman, as if her spirit was broken.

"Somebody's for sure been stealin' cattle from aroun' here," she said. "But it ain't my boys!" She looked into Maggie's eyes with such sadness, Maggie felt her own eyes smarting.

"I know it isn't, Mrs. MacKenna," she said. "And Pa knows it and Mr. Trent knows it. Don't you worry. We'll find the real crooks." She spoke with more confidence than she felt, because the old woman had no theories. There was nothing to go on.

As Maggie rode out of the wooded hills that bordered the lake, on impulse she turned Penny off the trail. She rode through the long prairie grasses along the hills to the east. She had never been here before, and it was very beautiful, with big empty wheat fields to her left, and the hills studded with oaks and poplars to her right. Something jumped up in the grass right in front of her. Penny shied, frightened. Maggie managed to stay on. She pulled the horse to a stop and smiled as a half-grown fawn ran toward the woods. It was so delicate, so vulnerable somehow, that it brought a lump to her throat. A doe with large liquid eyes came to meet it, nosed it, then they both ran, white tails flashing as they disappeared in the woods.

Maggie came to the creek, and the fording place where the road crossed it. She crossed the creek and the trail, heading east all the time. She had just decided she had better turn for home when she noticed something strange. Some of the long grasses ahead were trampled flat. There was a wide path, leading from the stubble field toward the woods. Pa hadn't mentioned a homestead on this side of the lake, but whoever lived around here might have some information about the cattle thefts. She decided to find out.

The path led into the woods. The horse was walking now, carefully, picking her way between the trees toward the lake. Maggie heard voices. She tied Penny to a tree and went forward on foot.

First she saw the lake glimmering through the trees. Then she saw a fire on the bank. There were five or six men in dark clothes sitting around the fire, eating. They looked like cowboys, with big-brimmed hats and high leather boots not at all like the laced-up workboots the homesteaders wore. She crept forward, hoping to be able to make out who these strange men were. What she saw stopped her in her tracks.

There, behind the men, among the trees was a corral filled with horses. There must have been twenty or thirty. They were all colours, and they looked straggly, not carefully groomed like her horses.

Over the fire was a huge spit holding a leg of beef. The men were eating the roasted meat with their fingers. One man went to the spit and cut off a chunk, his knife flashing in a ray of sunlight.

These men must be the cattle thieves! And horse thieves, too, by the look of it. Maggie was excited. She'd ride to town and tell Pa, then he'd tell the Mounties and everything would be all right soon!

She turned to hurry back to Penny, and stopped dead. Barring her way was a huge man in dark clothes, scowling out from the shade of his big cowboy hat.

"Well, well, young lady," he said. "How did you get out of the cave? I don't think the boss is goin' to like you tryin' to go off like this. I don't think he'll like it at all!"

And with that, he grabbed her arm and dragged her down the hill toward the men around the fire. "See what I found," he shouted.

The men glanced toward them, and Maggie, frightened as she was, couldn't help but notice the look of shock on their faces.

"How did you get away so fast?" spluttered one of the men. "I jis saw you back there inside the hill." Then he hurried into the dark mouth of a cave which seemed to have been dug into the bank, with a big pile of earth near its mouth. In a moment he was back with a slight girl wearing a green print dress. She had long brown hair. Maggie felt like she was looking into a mirror as she stared at the girl's face. It was her face. She knew instantly who it was. It seemed impossible, but it must be. This was Ellie. The real Ellie Trenholme.

• • •

The Ebenezer family had gone to town for the day. Nicholas asked politely if he could please go with them. He wanted to go to visit the boot-and-harness shop, but Newt told him he had to stay behind to milk the cows.

When they had gone, Nicholas realized he was absolutely alone. It was broad daylight, he didn't have to worry about the cows for a few hours, and there was no one there to watch his every move. So much of the time he felt like a prisoner, he was lightheaded with excitement over a free day!

He ran toward the Trenholmes' place, hoping to find Maggie there. He hadn't told her yet about his struggles to conquer his fear of horses. He wanted to show her how well he had learned to ride.

No one was home. Probably the family had all gone to the ball game in Valhalla, he thought. Then he checked the barn. The work team was gone and Copper was alone in his stall. Nicholas knew at once what that meant: Maggie was riding Penny out on the prairie. He would find her and surprise her!

He gave Copper his head, and the gelding ran flat out across the prairie. Nicholas rode now with skill and confidence. He felt the wind blowing through his hair and Copper's muscles rippling under his chestnut coat. The boy leaned forward, his body moving easily with the rhythm of the galloping horse. He laughed aloud.

Copper was running southward. Nicholas knew that the two horses hated to be separated, so he figured Copper was following Penny. He didn't try to turn Copper until the gelding entered the woods on the hills that surrounded Boulder Lake. He couldn't believe that Copper would have been able to follow Penny such a long distance from home, and he couldn't believe that Maggie would have come to this place. But Copper took the bit in his teeth and plunged into the trees.

Sure enough, there was Penny, tied to a tree. Nicholas slipped off Copper and tied him beside her. He could hear voices and walked toward them.

Below him, milling around on the banks of the lake, was a group of dangerous-looking men. They seemed to be arguing. Most of them had guns, and some had knives stuck into their belts. And in their midst, sitting on a boulder with her arms and feet tied with a rope, like a trussed sheep, was Maggie!

Nicholas froze, his mind racing. What should he do? Behind Maggie, hanging from the branch of a tree, was a red and white hide. Nicholas recognized it at once. It was the hide of the Ebenezers' stolen heifer. He knew it well, for all the cattle he cared for were like his friends. He felt more angry than frightened.

One of the men below shouted for silence. The other men seemed scared of him, and they quietened down immediately. "Sure, Bill," one said. "We're listening."

"I've made up my mind," said Bill. "We'll have to get rid of the girls. It's time to move on."

"I say we let them both go," said one of the other men. "When we first got here, it seemed like a good idea to take a hostage in case the marshals, or whatever you call them up here, came after us. But these farmers are so dumb they likely haven't noticed they've been supplyin' us with fresh beef. They haven't even noticed that we've been holdin' one of their own as hostage. We've been hidin' out for weeks and haven't seen hide nor hair of no one."

"Shut up, Gulliver!" growled Bill. "Ya don't know what yur talkin' about. Nobody's bothered us 'cause nobody knows we're here. This is the best hideout we've ever had. Nobody lives on this side of the lake, so no traffic goes by. I was hopin' to hole up here 'til spring, then make tracks out west and get us into the horse trade there."

The men laughed at this and one said, "Good plan, Bill."

"Nobody's heard of us out west," said another. "It'd be easy pickin's there, I reckon."

"Things have changed!" shouted Bill. "Are ya all so bone-headed ya cain't see it? We're holdin' two young'uns now, steada one. Twins, I reckon. The new one musta come lookin' fer her sister. It'll be jis a matter of time 'til their folks, or the Mounted Police, or both, come a-lookin' for 'em. They might be young, but they could tell the police a whole lot about us. It's best t'git ridda 'em, then make tracks."

"We can take them away from here, then let them go in some place faraway," said Gulliver.

Bill looked disgusted. "You don't think anybody'd notice a gang chasin' a buncha horses with two youngsters ridin' alongside? Seems to me, that's askin' for trouble. I say we should get ridda both them girls, then take off."

Some of the men gathered silently around Gulliver and some around Bill as they argued back and forth. "Last time I looked, I was still the boss around here," said Bill. "Anybody wanta argue the fact?"

He was staring at Gulliver as he said this and his thumbs were hooked into his belt.

Nicholas had to think. He had no idea who the other girl was they were talking about, but that was definitely Maggie down there with that gang of thieves. If he ran down to save her, he would soon be tied like she was, and that wouldn't do any good. No, his only hope was to ride for help. And he had to be quick about it. He knew that Maggie's life depended on him and him alone.

He realized that it would be unlikely anyone would notice him in all the noisy arguing, so he ran full tilt back to Copper. But he knew that if he left Penny and took Copper, the horses would make a fuss. The last thing he wanted was a neighing horse to signal those thieves that there was someone in the woods. He untied both horses, sprang onto Copper's back and galloped away, with Penny thudding along at Copper's side.

There was no point in going to any of the nearby farms. It was likely the farmers were all in town for the day. So he decided to ride directly to Valhalla. He figured that would be a ride of anywhere from twelve to fifteen miles. It would take hours to get there and back!

Nicholas rode on, mile after mile. He grew hot and tired, and there was a sharp pain in his side, but he knew he couldn't stop and rest. Then he noticed that Copper was slowing his pace. The gelding was still labouring to keep up his speed, but he had already had a hard ride that afternoon. His skin was slick with sweat, and foam was blowing from his mouth back into the boy's eyes.

Nicholas pulled up at the edge of a slough where the horses could drink and catch their breath. They skidded to a stop on its bank, both blowing hard. Nicholas smelled the fetid water as soon as they stopped. He had forgotten how brackish the water had become in the hot, dry weather. Penny nosed the green scum and swung her head up without drinking. Copper lipped the water, then he backed away. Nicholas wished he had watered them a few miles back, when they crossed the creek. Too late to think of that now!

The boy sprang to Penny's back, urging her forward in a full gallop. Copper, free of a rider now, was able to match her pace.

They were a strange sight as they burst into town, the English boy, his cheeks red and his eyes burning, the chestnut horses both galloping full tilt with lathered coats and bursting hearts.

The ball game and bazaar were over, but most country people had gathered to see the train come in before leaving for home.

Nicholas rode toward the crowd on the station platform. Pa ran to meet him. Nicholas fell from Penny and would have collapsed if Pa hadn't led him to a bench.

In a minute, Nicholas had enough breath to tell what had happened.

"Ellie!" screamed Mrs. Trenholme, when she heard Nicholas' story.

"Ellie and some other girl," explained Nicholas. "I didn't see the other one, but the bandits were talking about holding two girls hostage."

The Mountie had just got on the train, but he was hastily brought to Nicholas, where he asked many questions. "I'll get some fresh horses at the livery stable," he said. "Do you think you could lead the way to this camp?" Nicholas nodded.

Someone brought Nicholas a drink of water and a leftover sandwich from a picnic basket while the Mountie took Penny and Copper to be cared for at the livery stable. Within a half-hour, the policeman, Nicholas and Dan Trent had fresh mounts and were ready to go. Just as they were leaving, Asa Ebenezer rode up on a frisky young horse. Nicholas looked at him in surprise.

"My dad's done enough harm," Asa said. "I want to do somethin' to help out." He looked right at his father as he spoke. "I'm not goin' to go along with what you say anymore. You can try to beat me if you want to, but I'm 'most big as you are now."

"We don't have time to talk," said the Mountie. "You can come, but only if you do what you're told."

Pa told Nicholas that he had to take Mother home, and they would wait there for him and Ellie.

And with that, the Mountie and his informal gang of deputies rode out of town. They followed Nicholas directly across the prairie and through stubble fields. When they neared the Trenholme farm, Dan Trent galloped over to the empty house and came back carrying Pa's rifle.

After a hard ride, they arrived at the lake. They left their horses in the trees and crept stealthily toward the cave, with Nicholas leading the way. Nicholas raised his hand and they halted and surveyed the scene below on the bank of the lake. The gang was getting ready to make its getaway. Their horses were saddled and there were rolls tied behind each saddle. Some men were loading a couple of pack horses with bundles. Nicholas could see the long handle of a frying pan protruding from a pack. The men who weren't working were pacing around. They seemed agitated, Nicholas thought. Then a man rode into the camp from the far side.

"I followed one of 'em, then she got away," he said. "I looked everywhere, but she got clean away."

"The strangest thing," he went on. "First there were the two of 'em runnin' through the trees, then there was one, then they both jus' disappeared inta thin air."

"Next time there's somethin' important to do, I'll do it myself," growled Bill. "You're useless! You let yourself be outwitted by two skinny little things, not half your size."

The man had dismounted and was standing in front of Bill, turning his hat in his hands. He seemed to be watching Bill's right arm. Bill's gun hung from the right side of his belt.

While this was going on, the Mountie motioned Dan Trent to circle around the other side of the gang. Mr. Trent silently disappeared into the trees. The Mountie whispered to Asa and Nicholas to stay with the horses, then he quietly began circling in the other direction from Mr. Trent.

In a moment, Nicholas heard a shout from the Mountie and saw him in his bright red coat on the lake shore. The thieves were so taken by surprise, they didn't even try to draw their guns. Dan Trent came out of the trees with his rifle as Bill swung around, looking for a way to escape,

"Now draw your guns real easy," said the Mountie, "and toss them over here."

The gang gave up at once. The Mountie held a gun on the men while Mr. Trent cut lengths of rope and tied their hands behind their backs. When he came to Gulliver, the outlaw suddenly grabbed him by the arm and tried to pull him in front of him. Dan Trent gave a roar and broke away. The Mountie fired a warning shot, and in a moment Gulliver was under control.

As they tied up Gulliver, Nicholas scanned the scene and realized that Bill had disappeared. He must have sneaked into the trees while the Mountie and Mr. Trent were concentrating on capturing Gulliver. Then Nicholas heard a sound coming from behind some shrubbery. There was a muffled cracking sound like someone stepping on dry twigs. Asa was standing obediently holding the horses, so it wasn't him. Nicholas picked up a thick branch and waited.

First he saw a black hat, then a figure coming toward him. It was Bill, the leader of the gang. He was trying to make his way quietly while keeping an eye on what was going on below, so he didn't see Nicholas swing the branch.

By the time the Mountie responded to Nicholas' shout and bounded up the hill, Bill was lying in a crumpled heap, unconscious, and the boy was standing over him, the branch still in his hand.

On the way back to town, Nicholas turned off at the Trenholmes' farm. He was the one who had to bring the news that the deputies had looked through the woods around the camp, and called and called, but Ellie Trenholme was nowhere to be found.

Chapter Twenty-One

The Mystery of Ellie

A little later, Nicholas was sitting at the table in the Trenholmes' kitchen. Pa had just said, "I'll get some of the neighbours and we'll find our Ellie. Don't worry, Mother." He pulled on his hat, and when he opened the door to go out, Maggie was standing there. She looked exhausted and dishevelled, her dress badly torn and dirty.

The next few minutes were noisy and confusing as they hugged one another, and everyone talked at once. Finally, Maggie started her story again, and they listened quietly.

The leader of the thieves was called Bill Bristol. She had been tied up with her back against a boulder. The gang seemed to forget about her while they argued among themselves about what to do with her and another hostage being held in a cave they had dug into the hillside. While they were arguing, she noticed that one had carelessly dropped his knife with his half-eaten chunk of meat. So near, but yet so far.

Some of the gang wanted to let her go, while others said that would be too dangerous. One had argued that the smart thing to do would be to let her go in some distant place, and by the time the Mounties got her story, the gang would be safely hidden somewhere else. She didn't tell Pa and Mother that Bill Bristol had wanted to kill the hostages, because she was afraid of upsetting Mother even more than she already was.

At one point, all the men disappeared inside the cave. While she was alone, she had the chance to roll away from the boulder and get hold of the knife. She just had time to roll back into position, with the knife jammed behind her against the rock, before one of the men came out of the cave. Then Bill came out and said he'd like to get away before dark. The men saddled up and most of them rode off in different directions to see if the coast was clear. The man left behind as guard went over to his horse, a big handsome bay, tethered on the other side of the corral, and began grooming it. While he was busy, Maggie was able to work her ropes against the knife blade until at last she was free. Then, she escaped into the woods and walked around the lake until she came to the MacKennas' place. There was no one there, so she borrowed a horse and rode home.

"I hope they won't mind that I took their horse," she said. "I didn't think I had the strength to walk all the way home."

"Marie won't mind, lassie," said Pa. "She'll be happy as a meadowlark in spring that you helped clear her boys."

Only then did Mother notice that one of Maggie's fingers was wrapped in a strip torn from her dress. She had cut it deeply while freeing herself from the ropes. Mother got a basin of water and a proper bandage while Nicholas filled them in on what he had learned.

The Mountie had told Nicholas that Bill Bristol and his gang were wanted for stealing horses in the United States.

They were being chased by some U.S. marshals when they escaped across the border and had been hiding out at Boulder Lake ever since.

The Mountie would wait in Valhalla for reinforcements, then the thieves would be escorted to the American border and handed over to the authorities there. He said that he was glad to have Dan Trent and Asa along to help. He also said that, if it hadn't been for Ellie discovering the hideout and Nicholas for leading him there, then capturing Bill Bristol himself, the gang might not have been caught for months, or even years.

Pa laughed out loud when he heard this. "I couldn't be more proud of you both," he said.

Nicholas excused himself. He had to get back to the Ebenezers'. After he left, Mother stood up and walked to where Maggie was sitting.

"Well, I'm not proud," she said, and her voice was shrill and angry. "I asked you not to do anything dangerous, and you go and get yourself caught by a gang of thieving desperadoes."

"Now, now, Mother," said Pa soothingly.

"I want you to learn," said Mother to Maggie. "I want you to learn to listen to what I say! You're a foolish, foolish girl!"

Maggie stared at her, her face pale and startled. Suddenly she burst into tears and ran into the night.

She headed for her place of refuge, the barn, and threw herself into a pile of clean straw, sobbing as though her heart was breaking. She had been terrified and exhausted, and, instead of comforting her, Mother had attacked her.

She didn't hear Pa coming in, but she felt his big hand on her shoulder. "There, there, lassie," he said. "Your mother's had a big fright and she's not thinkin' straight. She'll see it different in the morning after we've all had a good night's sleep."

"Oh, Pa," said Maggie, her voice shaking. "I try so hard, but she's always cross with me. She doesn't want me to do anything on my own. She treats me like a baby."

"I think there's somethin' you need to know about Mother," said Pa. "Ellie, lass, you're the fifth baby Mother had. The fifth baby and the only one that lived. I know she sounds harsh, Ellie, but it's only because she's afraid somethin' will happen to you too. You're the only one she's got, you see."

Maggie stopped crying and took in this new information. It explained so many things about Mother. Then she put her head on Pa's shoulder and cried a little more because she was too tired not to.

The next day Maggie wanted to be alone to think. She wandered along the creek bank until she came to Ellie's grandpa's grave. She sat there for a while thinking about the hard life of the pioneers, before modern hospitals and doctors who could save little babies.

But uppermost in her mind was the part of her story she hadn't told Mother and Pa. After the guard had brushed his horse, he led it down to the lake and began washing it. When he was occupied, she had cut the rope that bound her wrists. She took the knife with her as she crawled on her hands and knees on the stony ground to the cave, all the while keeping watch on the guard from the corner of her eye. Inside the cave it was black-dark until her eyes adjusted, then she saw Ellie.

She motioned for Ellie to be quiet, then she quickly freed the girl. There were a million things Maggie wanted to ask, but first they had to escape. The two girls were running through the woods, their long brown hair swinging, when they heard the man on horseback shouting at them.

"We've got to separate," Maggie gasped. "He can't go two ways at once." Then she turned sharply and plunged into the thick growth.

She had told Pa and Mother the rest of her story. She had walked to the MacKennas' and borrowed a horse. She had no idea what had happened to the real Ellie, although Nicholas had said that both hostages had escaped.

She sat on by Ellie's grandpa's grave for a long time, wondering if the real Ellie Trenholme was still in the woods by Boulder Lake. And, if she was, how long would it be before she came home?

Chapter Twenty-Two

Winter

For weeks, whenever someone came to the door, Maggie was sure it was Ellie. But, when Ellie didn't appear, she began to doubt that she had actually seen anyone in the cave. She had been so frightened, perhaps her imagination had gotten the better of her.

Now that she understood Mother better, she felt quite happy and satisfied with life. She didn't want to leave Manitoba. Not just yet. Not until Nicholas was settled with his mother. But she realized that, if Ellie ever did come back, she would have no choice.

November and still no snow. The ground was frozen hard, and everyone had to bundle up before going outside. The kitchen in the little log farmhouse was cosy with the cookstove burning all day long, but Maggie was very cold in her make-shift room. Mother had all her extra household utensils stored in one corner now, and Maggie had hung some pictures from old calendars on the walls. The one she liked best was a bridge over a stream bordered with trees covered with white blossoms. A beautiful woman in a pink dress was driving a white horse hitched to a blue cart across the bridge. The reins were blue ribbons, and the horse had flowers woven into its mane.

But even though the room now seemed more like a bedroom than a storage shed, Maggie was still miserable. She had to leave the door open so heat could come in from the kitchen, but it didn't do much good. Pa said he hoped they'd get snow before the cold weather came. Maggie, shivering, wondered if this was a joke she couldn't understand.

One day Pa said he had a present for her. He had gone to town with the wagon that morning, and bought a tiny iron stove called a heater. He spent the afternoon hooking stovepipes together and fixing them into a chimney which had been built for the cookstove when Maggie's bedroom was used as a back kitchen in hot summers.

With the new stove in place, Maggie was able to build a fire in the evening to take the chill off her room. It was such a small heater, with so little capacity for wood, that the fire didn't last long after she went to bed. In the morning, Mother built a fire before Maggie woke, so the room was bearable when it was time to get dressed. Still, even with the heater, Maggie couldn't leave water in the jug on her dresser or it would freeze in the night.

Miss Fieldmont said she was quite comfortable in her room. The cookstove in the kitchen backed onto the wall of her room, and the stovepipe came through the wall and angled across the ceiling before going up into the chimney. This was done so the heat from the stovepipes wouldn't be wasted. Mother and Pa's room was the coldest in the house, but they never complained.

One day, Newt Ebenezer drove into the yard. Nicholas had only been in school a few days that month, and at first Maggie hoped Newt was there to say he'd let the boy come back to school for the winter. Or, even better, that the boy's mother was coming from England. But, instead of asking to speak to Pa, Newt talked to Mother on the doorstep for a few minutes, then he left. Mother came into the house, and told Maggie that Matilda Ebenezer was "sick." She didn't know how long she'd be away, but she gave Maggie instructions for preparing meals for the rest of the day. Then she went to the barn to harness Penny and Copper. Before she left, she came back to the house, went into her bedroom and came out with a bundle wrapped in a sheet.

Maggie was sure that Matilda Ebenezer was having her baby, and wondered that Mother wouldn't talk about it in front of her. Apparently, in the nineteenth century, a girl her age was considered too young to know about such things.

That afternoon, while Matilda Ebenezer was giving birth, the first snowstorm of the year hit. When Maggie went to the well for a pail of water, the yard and the buildings were covered with a layer of white and the snow was granular beneath her feet. Mother was back by supper time. The new baby was another girl. "Poor little mite," Mother said. "Another mouth to feed and she's not too welcome. Newt is beside himself. He'd been hoping so hard for a boy to help with the farm work."

That night, the wind blew and howled around the little house. In the morning a blizzard was raging. The air was thick with snow, so nothing was visible. The water was frozen in the kettle on the stove. The fearful wind blew into every crack and cranny of the house.

Pa had to go out in the storm to milk the cows and feed all of the animals. When he got back, he was blown in the door, a snowman, with black holes for eyes glimmering between swathes of a huge scarf. In his hands were clutched the handles of two milk pails. When Mother pried them from his stiffened hands, Maggie could see that most of the milk had blown against Pa's legs, which were now crusted with white.

Mother and Miss Fieldmont pulled the table near the stove at their noon meal. They ate hot soup and shivered in their heavy jackets, even while they sipped from their steaming bowls. Pa said it was too bad he hadn't got the house banked before winter struck. Maggie decided not to ask what banking a house was. She figured she'd find out soon enough.

For three days the blizzard did not let up. Pa was the only one who ventured outside. On the first day, he had rounded up the calves and put them in the barn. They had been outside, in the shelter of a straw stack, all but Dora's black and white calf. He hadn't worried too much, saying the little bull calf would come in by himself from wherever he was. But the calf hadn't come.

Maggie could tell that, when Pa used his warm breath to melt a hole in the frost on the window and stood staring out at the blowing snow, he was thinking of that half-grown calf out in that awful storm. Maggie knew that, if it was lost, this would be another big loss. But she knew that Pa really cared for each animal on the farm, so he was worried about more than losing money.

They kept the coal-oil lamp burning all day so they could see well enough to sew and knit. Mother was making heavy grey mittens, and Miss Fieldmont was doing some delicate embroidered birds and butterflies on some pillowcases. Maggie sat by the lamp reading aloud. Miss Fieldmont had brought *Oliver Twist* by Charles Dickens out of her trunk, and Mother said they were lucky to have a book written by a man so long-winded. It could storm every day 'til spring and they'd still not be finished the story.

On the fourth day, the wind had gone and the sun shone again. Pa hitched Penny and Copper to a neat little cutter with curving runners for Maggie and Miss Fieldmont to drive to school. Maggie felt as though she was riding on Santa Claus' sled. This would not be a new experience for Ellie, so Maggie couldn't show her surprise and delight.

Miss Fieldmont and Maggie looked at each other and laughed. Their faces were barely visible through the scarves that Mother had wound around their heads. The teacher tucked a horsehide robe over their knees, and Maggie clucked her tongue at the chestnut horses. Penny and Copper hadn't had any exercise for three days, so they dashed off over the frozen snow, making Maggie and the teacher laugh again with the fun of it all.

When they got home from school in the afternoon, Maggie realized what banking the house meant. Pa had piled snow against all sides of the building, all around the floor line, to keep out drafts. The house was warmer after this. It was still freezing cold in the mornings, and always when the wind blew. But the floor was warmer, so if you spilled water you could wipe it up before it froze. Mother said that, when they got their new house next year, it would be built so tight, not a whisper of cold air would blow in.

When Pa came in from the barn, he had bad news. He had ridden Belle out onto their pasture land and had found Dora's calf. It had frozen to death during the storm. Pa said he might not have found it until spring, but for the fact that one black and white leg was sticking up through a snowbank.

That night, they went to bed hearing the long mournful howls of prairie wolves floating on the frosty air. The wolves had found the carcass of the calf and were feasting on the moonlit prairie. Maggie pulled the covers over her head, then she put her hands over her ears. She went to sleep finally, those fiendish howls in her ears, wishing she were anywhere else but in this harsh, desolate place.

•••

Miss Fieldmont trained her students all month for the Christmas Concert on December 23. Pa had been to town that morning and when he came home he looked peculiar; like the cat that ate the canary, as Mother said. But he refused to answer when Maggie tugged at his sleeve and begged him to tell what he'd been doing in town. When it was time to go to the concert, he went to the barn to hitch Penny and Copper to the sleigh. Miss Fieldmont, Mother and Maggie were bundling themselves into their heavy coats when they heard the sound of little bells. The gay jingling carried on the frosty air was the sweetest music Maggie had ever heard. Then the sound stopped.

They went outside to see what was going on. The evening was bright with moon and stars, so they could see the outlines of horses and sleigh. Just then Penny looked toward them and tossed her head. The bells rang out, then were still. Maggie ran to her horses.

Both had new bridles, featuring a beautiful brass medallion between their eyes. And, fastened to their harnesses were strings of bells.

Pa laughed at Maggie's speechlessness. "It's the first time you've been short of words, lassie. This is my Christmas present for all of you. That old harness never fit this team somehow, wasn't good enough for these high-steppers. So, I had Fridbjorn make us a new set. You'll see it better in daylight, but this is harness worthy of a pretty little team of drivers."

Mother, Maggie and Miss Fieldmont sat in the bottom of the sleigh on a thick cushion of clean straw. They had horsehair and buffalo robes tucked around them. Maggie looked up at the night sky studded with stars. All the way to Victoria

School, as Penny and Copper pranced and danced across the hard prairie snow, their bells rang out, letting the whole world know that it was Christmas time, the happiest time of the year.

The school was transformed. Coal-oil lamps shone in holders at intervals along the walls, casting a soft yellow light on the scene. A huge Christmas tree had been brought from the Sand Hills earlier in the week. It was standing in the corner and was decorated with bits of white paper cut into snowflakes by the students, wound with strings of red rosehips which had been gathered weeks before, and it was topped with a silver star snipped from a piece of tin.

Everyone from miles around piled into the schoolhouse. The desks were saved for the ladies, while the men and children sat on coats along the walls, or stood at the back. The Ebenezers came late, and Maggie was disappointed, but not surprised, to see that Nicholas was not with them.

A wash boiler full of coffee was set to simmer on the stove for later on, and the show began.

And what a show it was! The girls danced the Highland fling, and the boys danced the sailors' hornpipe. Boys and girls together performed an elaborate drill in which they marched and halted and turned and wheeled, all the while making patterns by raising and lowering Union Jacks. Then there was a humorous play called "The Parson's Visit" and several recitations of long, involved rhyming stories. The evening ended with the students singing all the songs they had learned that fall, with Miss Fieldmont directing with her smart little baton.

While the students were singing, little Mary Brown, always so shy, hung her head and twisted her skirt with one hand. Maggie was horrified as the hem of Mary's skirt rose higher and higher as she twisted it, first above her knees revealing her brown knit stockings, then higher, until her heavy pink flannel underwear was showing. There was a gasp from the crowd and Maggie saw Mary's mother bending forward in an agony of embarrassment. Maggie leaned down and took Mary's hand, letting the hem fall to its normal place. The crowd chuckled in relief.

At the end of the concert there was so much applause and shouting and whistles that Miss Fieldmont agreed to repeat the flag drill.

Then there was lunch. As people ate and chatted, Maggie heard over and over comments about what a fine concert it had been. They judged the teacher by the quality of her concert, and this was her final acceptance into the community.

On the way home, as Penny's and Copper's bells jingled in the night air, Miss Fieldmont, who was very excited about her success, squeezed Maggie's hand and asked her if she could ever be happier than she was tonight.

Maggie didn't say anything. She was thinking of Nicholas and wondering why he wasn't at the concert. She had to find a way to see him.

In the days before the concert, Mother had prepared the little log house for Christmas. First, all the furniture had to be pulled to the middle of the kitchen so she could give the walls a fresh coat of whitewash. When that was done, the curtains were taken down, washed and ironed. There was no Christmas tree, but for a few cents Pa bought boughs cut from the bottoms of the trees for sale in Valhalla. He fixed them over the doors and windows. Their fresh scent perfumed the air.

Mother's hens weren't laying much in the cold weather, so all the eggs Maggie found when she slipped her hand under their warm feathered bodies were used for baking. There weren't enough for Pa to have his favourite fried eggs for breakfast. But cakes and pies were piling up in the storage cupboard in Maggie's room.

Maggie worked at noon hour at school making her Christmas gifts. She knit a pair of gloves for Pa to wear when the weather warmed up enough for gloves instead of big double mitts. She was using scraps of knitting wool, so each finger was a different colour. She thought they looked very beautiful.

Miss Fieldmont had been teaching the girls to crochet all fall. Maggie had almost finished a delicate, lacy white dress and matching hat, big enough for a small doll. When she had them finished, she soaked them in sugar and water, so they dried stiff. Then she made a doll's head of a ball of white yarn, with yellow yarn hair and features stitched with black thread. By the time she had her doll put together, with an inner framework of stiff paper, she thought it was beautiful. It was a present for Mother.

On Christmas Eve, Pa killed the goose that Mother had been fattening all fall for the Christmas feast. Mother laid the plucked bird on the table and then made an incision so she could remove its innards. Maggie watched while Mother plunged her hand into the bird and pulled out the slimy intestines, which she threw in the pail for the pigs as a special treat. When all the other innards were lying on the table, she went through them, picking out the parts they would cook for the feast. There was the shiny liver, and the rubbery gizzard, which she slit open and cleaned out. There was the heart, unmistakable in its shape, but what was that big lump covered with a membrane?

"I think we're lucky," said Mother. She cut through the membrane, revealing a big white goose egg streaked with blood. Mother wiped it off with a cloth. "This is the egg it would have laid if it'd lived another day," she said. "Now your pa will have a special treat for his breakfast on Christmas morning."

On Christmas morning the sun shone and the wind was still. Mother stuffed the goose and put it in the oven as soon as she got up. After the animals had been cared for, the family ate breakfast together. Pa chuckled with delight when Maggie handed him his plate piled high with fried potatoes, strips of crisp bacon and the biggest fried egg she had ever seen.

After breakfast, the family gathered around the kitchen table to open their gifts. When Pa opened his present from Maggie, he was speechless. Then he recovered and declared they were the finest gloves he'd ever seen. The only problem he could see was that all the other men in the district would want some just like them, and he didn't know where she'd find the time to make them all.

Mother and Maggie had picked out the teacher's gift at Candle's. It was a picture frame decorated in the corners with carved roses. "We got it for you to frame a picture of your parents," said Maggie. Miss Fieldmont thanked them, then she gave Maggie and Mother both a hug and thanked them again.

Mother gave Pa what Maggie would call a sweater, but they called it a knitted coat. She had knit Maggie a warm green hood with matching mittens.

Miss Fieldmont gave Pa a good strong hammer. Mother and Maggie each got a length of soft cashmere for new dresses. Mother's was navy blue, with silver buttons, and Maggie's was crimson, with brass buttons and black braid. She had never seen anything so beautiful. "It's too much," said Mother, gently stroking the soft fabric. "Oh, it's too much."

"No, my friends," said Miss Fieldmont softly. "You have given me a real home. I only wish I could give you more."

Pa had already given the new harness as a Christmas present, so he went to the barn, and the women began to prepare the feast.

When Miss Fieldmont left to walk across the fields to meet Mr. Phillips-Jones, who was coming for Christmas dinner, Maggie was finally alone with Mother. She shyly gave Mother her present.

When Mother saw her crocheted doll, she didn't say anything for a long time. With one finger she traced the rim of the little hat and down the front of the lace dress.

"I've never had anything so pretty," she said. "Not in my whole life. Is it to put on my dresser?"

"For now," said Maggie. "But when you get your new house, I want you to put it on your sideboard."

Mother looked at Maggie, her eyes shining.

"Mother," said Maggie, "I want to tell you something. I think you know it, but I want to say it out loud." She took a deep breath. "Mother, I just want you to know that I love you and Pa."

Mother's face started to crumple, then she reached out and took Maggie in her strong sinewy arms. "We're told to love one another. The Good Book tells us that. But, it's hard to say. Sometimes the hardest thing in the world. I ..." and she paused as if to get the strength to say it. Maggie felt her body stiffen with the effort, and when she spoke her voice was husky as she said simply, "You're my daughter. You're all I've got."

Maggie knew that this was all Mother could bring herself to say, but she also knew that it was because Mother's feelings were so strong that she couldn't say more.

"Don't say I'm all you've got," said Maggie, wondering again what had happened to the real Ellie. "You've got Pa," she said,

"Yes," said Mother, brushing a few strands of long hair back from Maggie's face. "I've got a lot to be thankful for. I've got you, and I've got your pa. But nothing lasts forever. If I ever lose you, I'll find comfort in today, the day we told each other right out how we feel about each other." Then she quickly passed her sleeve over her face, cleared her throat and went back to work.

It was a happy Christmas dinner. The goose was crisp, the gravy rich, the plum pudding a work of art. But what Maggie remembered in the years after was Pa's cheerful good nature, and the fact that Mother had let her know that she loved her. Maggie knew it was Ellie she loved, but in a way that meant Maggie was loved too.

The winter dragged on, as if it would last forever. There was not as much snow as Maggie was used to, but the cold was more bitter and intense than any she had ever known. Maggie thought often about the real Ellie. She hoped that, wherever she was, she was safe and warm.

All that long winter, when the weather allowed, there was either a dance or a card party in the school on Saturday nights. If there was a blizzard, the social would be cancelled, but if the thermometer dipped to thirty or forty degrees below zero, people just piled more robes over their laps, and heated stones in the oven to put at their feet. The horses were kept warm by the exercise of pulling the sleighs and cutters, but they had to be swathed in heavy horse blankets on arrival at the school.

Sometimes the Trenholmes went to the socials, sometimes they stayed home, but Miss Fieldmont never missed. Mr. Trent came regularly on Saturday afternoons with his elegant black drivers, and transported the teacher in style.

The minister didn't come out from town to preach in the winter, but Miss Fieldmont started a Sunday school, and those who lived nearest the school came on Sunday morning. Mr. Trent was always there, looking very distinguished in his black suit. Everyone wanted to be in his class. It was the only one where Bible study was punctuated with laughter.

One Sunday, Mr. Phillips-Jones approached the teacher and asked if she and the students of the Sunday school would be interested in coming to an evening of hymn singing once a week at his place. He had just bought a fine new organ for his little parlour, and he would like someone to make good use of it since he didn't play. From then on, Friday night was music night in the district.

Nicholas came to school once in a while. He stayed indoors at noon, catching up on his studies. He told Maggie that things were a little better. Asa seemed to admire Nicholas after he stood up to Newt, and even more so after his wild ride for help. He seemed to genuinely want to change his ways, and he appeared to want Nicholas to be his friend. He was even kind to Cora, now, and often helped her with her work.

But life was still harsh at the Ebenezers'. When it snowed, Nicholas woke to find the stuff had come in through the chinks in the roof and powdered his bed. Sometimes the moisture of his breath had frozen in the night, so the blankets stuck to his face. He never got enough to eat, so he was always tired and hungry. And even though Asa was changing, Newt was the same cruel bully he had always been.

When Maggie asked gently if he had had any word from his mother, he dropped his eyes and said in a small voice that, no, he had heard nothing. And it had been so long since he'd sent that letter to London that he feared the worst. He was afraid his mother had died.

Chapter Twenty-Three

Manitoba Crocus

Spring eventually came. Everyone seemed surprised, as if winter were the natural state of things. On a mild day when a soft wind was blowing from the south, and enough snow had melted to show patches of brown dead grass here and there, Pa bridled Copper for a ride and asked Maggie if she wanted to come along with him, so she hurried to bridle Penny.

The horses struggled across the pasture, their feet sinking in banks of snow softened by the spring sunshine. On grassy places they trotted a little, tossing their heads and snorting. Maggie was sure they were as excited by the sweet smell in the wind as she was. That wind promised green and growing and life on these prairies that had been frozen hard and dead for so long. She took a deep breath and let it out slowly. She smiled at Pa and he smiled back.

"I wanted to come out here to check the creek," he said.

Before they reached the creek, they could hear water running. When they reached the high bank and looked down, they could see the water was high and rushing along, carrying branches and debris with it.

"It's goin' to get higher yet. Might flood some of the pasture for a while," said Pa.

Maggie was mesmerized by the rushing water, but part of her was feeling a sharp sense of disappointment. She and Nicholas couldn't reach each other now, even if they had an excuse. The water was too high and dangerous to cross.

"I brought you out here to show you somethin' special," said Pa. And they rode the horses farther upstream, to Grandpa's grave. It was high enough that all the snow had melted around it. The grave and the brown grass around it, right down to the snowbanks in the surrounding hollow, were covered with a blanket of little purplish blue flowers.

"Crocuses," said Pa. "Good old Manitoba crocuses. Tough little devils. Come right up through the snow, before anythin' else gets the courage."

Maggie slid off Penny's back and bent down and slid her fingertips over one. The flowers were soft and furry, like velvet. "I guess crocuses are like Manitoba settlers, Pa," she said. "They're tough like us!"

Pa laughed. "You're right there, lassie. You have to be tough to make it in this country. Even so," he said, letting his gaze range across the prairie snow, then back to the creek and the grave surrounded by flowers. "Even so, I pity all the poor devils who live somewheres else."

When the snow went and the land dried, everyone was too busy for socializing, so the dances ended. The men went out on the land, sowing their crops with hopes for a profitable harvest. Mother was busy in her garden, hoeing and spading and planting. Maggie studied every free moment, hoping to pass her examinations so she could go to school in Valhalla in the fall with Kristjana. Miss Fieldmont was busy each evening sewing new clothes.

Mr. Trent was busiest of all. He hired carpenters from

Valhalla, and while he and his hired men planted his crop, the hammering of the builders rang out across the prairie. They were building his new house. Pa visited one day and came home to say that the house had two storeys, four bedrooms and a parlour. He couldn't figure why a bachelor needed so much room.

Then word got around that Mr. Phillips-Jones was also building a new house. He had hired some builders from Prairie Mound and they were constructing the largest and finest house yet seen in the district. It had three storeys, with rooms on the third floor for the hired girls he was going to need to keep the place clean. A load of fine oak had come on the train for the carpenters to build a curving staircase as well as mantels for all the heaters needed to keep the huge place warm in winter.

The carpenters said that Phillips-Jones was having them build a serving pantry between the kitchen and the dining room, with a little pass-through door so the cook could hand the food to the hired girls who'd be serving at the table.

"Dang-fool nonsense!" Pa scoffed. "He must think he still lives on some English estate."

Pa borrowed a big brown workhorse from Mr. Trent to work in the fields alongside Bess. When Maggie asked why he wasn't using Belle this spring, he said that she needed a little rest. Maggie didn't understand, but she had learned that asking questions when Pa didn't want to answer never got her anywhere.

One day, Maggie got her answer. Pa took her out on the prairie, this time to a poplar bluff. They tied Penny and Copper to a tree, and walked into the bluff, stepping over fallen trees. Finally they came to a clear space.

Pa stopped and gestured to Maggie to be quiet. Then he pointed. There, in a sheltered spot, hidden from everyone, was Belle, and beside her was a little black foal. Its legs were wobbly, and as it tried to walk the front legs buckled and it went down on its knees.

"Only a few hours old," said Pa. "I've been keepin' my eye on things, and I know there wasn't a little one this time yesterday."

Belle was licking her baby with her big rough tongue. Then she nosed it and snorted a little. The foal struggled to its feet. Belle moved, so it was in position to nurse. It spread its wobbly front legs and nosed under its mother until it found its dinner. Bits of frothy milk oozed out from the sides of its mouth. Belle turned her head to look at her baby, and nickered contentedly.

"A filly," said Pa. "We got us another little filly."

"Oh, Pa," said Maggie. "It's magic, isn't it?"

Pa smiled. "New life. Magic is a good enough word 'til a better comes along. Any ideas for a name for the filly, Ellie?"

"I think Crocus should be its name."

"Crocus?" he said, then he smiled at her. "You seem to have a knack for pickin' names, lassie. Crocus you say, and Crocus it will be."

When he finished putting in his crop, Mr. Trent and his hired men joined the builders in working on the house. Pa went over and helped for a few days, and several other neighbours did the same. Mr. Trent's goal was to complete the house by July 1. He planned to host a Dominion Day picnic on his farm for the whole district.

"Pa," said Maggie. "I haven't seen Nicholas for months. We've got to get him to the picnic."

"I agree with you there, lassie. I'll go over and have a word with Newt. Probably he wouldn't let his family go either, without a little persuasion."

Pa drove the buggy around by the road to the Ebenezers' farm, after supper. When he came home he sighed and said he'd done his best. They'd see when the day of the picnic came if his best was good enough.

Chapter Twenty-Four

Dominion Day Picnic

$\mathcal{O}$n the morning of the first of July, Mother and Pa had an argument about Ellie. Mother said she had enough work lined up for two. She had to make some of her molasses pies, get the picnic basket packed, pick some lettuce from the garden, iron Pa's good shirt and press her new dress. She couldn't do everything, she said, and needed Ellie's help.

Pa said he was sprucing up the drivers for the big day and that would take time, and he couldn't do everything by himself. "When you say it's time to leave, you expect everybody to snap to it," he said. "Well, if I have Ellie help me with the horses, I might just about be ready."

Maggie listened to them squabbling, then she went ahead and heated the irons on the stove, pressed Pa's shirt, picked and washed the lettuce and started cutting it up in a bowl with sour cream, mustard and sugar. Mother said Ellie was going through the work like grass through a goose. Finally Mother had her pies in the oven, and said she could see her way clear now, so why didn't Ellie get to the barn to see what Pa wanted.

Pa already had brushed Penny and Copper until they shone. He had combed their manes and tails with the big currycomb, and now he was braiding red, white and blue ribbons into Copper's long black mane. He showed Maggie how to do it, and she began braiding Penny's mane.

When the Trenholmes drove their buggy into Mr. Trent's front yard, Maggie felt proud to be seated between Mother, who was wearing the new brown poplin dress that she had finished sewing the night before, and Pa, who looked so dressed-up in his white shirt and dark suit, with his grey hair curling out from under his hat. Maggie was wearing the pink dress Mother had made last summer for school. They had turned the collar so a worn part was hidden. Its colour was now bright and new-looking, making the rest of the dress look quite faded. She would get a new dress in time for school in the fall.

Maggie was proudest of Penny and Copper tossing their tails and stepping high as if they realized how handsome they were in their custom-made harness with its fancy brass trim shining in the sun. The ribbons braided into their manes and the bells jingling on their backs gave them a festive air, as if they, too, were celebrating Canada's birthday.

As they drove up the lane, Maggie got her first close look at Dan Trent's new house. It was two storeys high with a veranda. It was built of lumber painted cream with green trim. The shingles were green and came down on the walls to the bottom of the upstairs windows. About midway down were a few rows of green and cream shingles interspersed in a checkerboard design. Maggie thought the house looked sturdy, comfortable and very pretty.

Over the front door, Mr. Trent had hung a huge Union Jack.

"Well, I've never seen anything so beautiful," said Mother, "You didn't tell me, Pa, that it was so fine."

"I tried to tell you," said Pa, "but I guess I didn't have the right words." Then Pa shook his head. "They're startin' to build houses like this here and there throughout the country-side. And Phillips-Jones' new house is far grander than all of 'em. I hope they don't live to regret spendin' so much on a place to lay their heads. Having a couple of good crops seems to addle some farmers' brains. They forget the hard times too fast."

"Ellie, Mrs. Trenholme," called Mr. Trent, waving from across the yard. "Bring your food over here."

Miss Fieldmont had been here since morning helping Mr. Trent set up planks on sawhorses under some trees, making a long table. The table was already loaded with sliced ham and roast beef; homemade buns and bread; blocks of butter with designs stamped into the top, making them look too perfect to spoil by cutting into them; potato salads and pickles. Mother put out her huge butter bowl of lettuce and took her pies down to the end of the table, where the desserts were.

The yard was ringed with buggies and wagons. The horses were tethered among the grove of young Manitoba maples that Mr. Trent had planted when he first took up his homestead. He said he had planted them on the north side of the yard to keep the winter winds from the house he knew even then he would some day build.

Maggie walked around, looking for Nicholas. At first she was afraid that Pa's best hadn't been good enough, and the Ebenezers hadn't come, then she saw them driving down the lane in their wagon, their old brown horses pulling it with their heads down as if their spirits had died long ago. Their flanks showed the remnants of caked manure, and their ribs showed that, like Nicholas, they were never given quite enough to eat.

But there on the seat beside Newt was Matilda Ebenezer looking pleased and excited, with the baby on her lap, and Cora and the two little girls standing behind her, hanging onto the sides of the bouncing wagon. Nicholas and Asa were sitting in the open back of the wagon box with their legs hanging down.

When everyone was finished eating, Mr. Trent brought out a box of oranges he had bought at Candle's and gave one to each child. They seldom saw such exotic fruit, and they were very excited. Then an even bigger surprise! Mr. Phillips-Jones had a small keg of luscious, store-bought chocolates. It was as if Christmas had come in July!

After the food was cleared away, the entertainment began. There were races for different age groups and a baseball game between the married men and the single men. Then came the part of the day that Maggie, when she went over her memories years later, thought was the best part of the celebration. The horse races!

The first race was for horses seventeen hands and over, so Penny and Copper had to wait. There were eight horses in the race, some ridden by boys, some by adults. But everyone knew the winner would be one of Mr. Trent's fine black drivers. He was riding one, and Miss Fieldmont, in a smart black riding habit, was riding side-saddle on the other. Mr. Phillips-Jones had come on his new horse, an elegant-looking bay, but after staring at Mr. Trent's drivers for some time he declined to enter the race.

Some men had volunteered to be spotters, and were already out on the prairie, half a mile away, to make sure all the entrants came the full distance before wheeling and galloping back to the starting position, which was also the finish line.

Mr. Trent's horses were pulling at their bits and pawing the ground until the sound of a dinner gong signalled the race had begun and they streaked across the prairie, the other six horses straggling behind. Maggie thought Miss Fieldmont was the most elegant rider she had ever seen, her slim body straight in the saddle, her gloved hands holding the reins in perfect position. Mr. Trent looked very handsome too, his horse's long legs eating up the ground. He got to the finish line just a stride or two behind the teacher. Miss Fieldmont, pink-cheeked and laughing, asked him why he had been holding his horse in. Didn't he think she would be able to win the race fair and square?

"That was a pretty sight," said Mother to Mrs. Archibald. "But not much of a horse race. I think the next one will be better."

It was time for the smaller horses to race. Maggie mounted Penny and rode across the yard to Nicholas and invited him to ride Copper. Newt Ebenezer scowled, but Nicholas paid no attention and ran to bridle the chestnut gelding. There were only four horses in this race, the Trenholmes' chestnuts, a fine-boned driver owned by Mrs. Archibald and ridden by her son, and an Indian pony, a pinto, owned and ridden by Billy Cranbrook. His father had bought it only a few months before, and it was still wild and only half-broken. All the young jockeys were riding bareback.

When the gong sounded, the horses shot away from the starting line. Maggie leaned forward into Penny's neck. She felt the ends of the braided ribbons as they whipped against her face. On her left, Copper was matching Penny's stride, pace for pace. On her right, she was aware of Billy Cranbrook on his pony. It wasn't as big as Penny and Copper, so she hoped it would not be able to cover the ground so quickly. But at the end of the half-mile, Billy and his half-wild pony were still neck and neck with the chestnuts.

As they wheeled and headed back to the farmyard, they met the Archibald's mare still coming, her rider shouting and whacking her flank with his hat. The three lead horses headed home with an explosion of speed. About halfway there, Billy pulled ahead on his pony. Maggie could see its white and brown head, then its side, then the white of its flank as it passed her. Billy glanced over his shoulder, but Penny's nose stayed even with his horse's flank, then she started to gain. He began to shout at his pony and, for the first time Maggie realized he was carrying a willow switch. As Penny and Copper pulled ahead, he lashed his pony with the switch, swinging great cutting blows across the pony's rump. Suddenly the poor animal broke its stride. It swung its head and reared.

Maggie and Nicholas swept to the finish line at almost exactly the same moment. She wasn't sure who had won, and no one was there to see, for the judges were running to Billy, who was picking himself up. His horse had thrown him and then run away across the prairie.

Luckily Billy wasn't hurt, but he was embarrassed, and soon the jokes started: Was he thinking of learning to ride soon? Had he been practising his stunts very long?

After all the excitement and exercise, people suddenly realized they were hungry again and they gathered at the table for more food before going home to milk the cows.

Maggie wandered away from the group. She went to Penny and Copper, tethered in the Manitoba maple grove. She always felt comforted by just being quiet with her beloved horses. She was worried about Nicholas. It looked certain now that he would have to stay with the Ebenezers until he was sixteen. She felt sad and helpless. She was standing there, rubbing Penny's neck, when she heard voices. She realized that Miss Fieldmont and Mr. Phillips-Jones were walking in the trees. She couldn't see them, and they couldn't see her, because Penny was between them and her. Mr. Phillips-Jones was speaking, his voice harsh and angry.

"But, why, when I can offer you so much more? You're a woman of breeding and education. What can you possibly see in someone who is such a …" He stopped speaking, searching for the word, and when it came to him, he spit it out with disdain. "Such a rustic!"

Then Maggie heard Miss Fieldmont's firm voice. "I know you're angry, Alfred, and I'm sorry. I should have told you long ago that I was having doubts about our — suitability. I know you have many advantages in life, and for a time I was blinded by them. You have something few homesteaders have — support from your family in time of need.

"Because of that you are building an impressive estate. And many would be happy for the chance to share it, Alfred. I'm sorry, but it's not for me."

"But, why, Catherine?"

"I have learned much about myself since I came to Manitoba. I've learned not to judge people by their wealth and achievements. The people I've come to love may be poor, but they have character. They keep their courage and keep going when things get difficult. Riches come and riches go, and goodness knows we all hope some will come our way, but character, Alfred, character is everything. I see that now."

Mr. Phillips-Jones' voice was dripping with sarcasm. "And you think this Trent fellow, with his simple-minded ideas, has what you call 'character'?"

Maggie heard no more, for the speakers had moved on. She felt suddenly very excited, and ran back to join the crowd.

Pa, as chairman of the school board, was standing on the veranda steps thanking Mr. Trent for his hospitality. Everyone clapped.

Then Mr. Trent stood on the steps of his fine new house and said a few words about Canada. "Canada is twenty-eight years old today. It doesn't have big cities like the old countries," he said, "but it has natural resources which will one day make us the envy of the world. And it has God-fearing people who have the stamina needed to develop a country like this."

He paused for a moment of polite applause, but he was warming up to his subject. "I tell you, ladies and gentlemen, we are fortunate to live in the finest land God ever created. And we are fortunate that we live in it now, when it is young. We will watch it grow into a great nation. I have a vision of the future. Canada won't be loved for its military, its ships and its guns. It will be loved because it gives ordinary people a chance to live good lives. The farmers and fishermen, the ordinary working people of our cities and towns, and all the Native peoples who lived here for thousands of years before us — we will build this country together, with our sweat and our brains. We are the pioneers. We will work on, in spite of hail and fire and grasshoppers and drought. We will succeed. We will build a country ruled not by guns, not by a gentry — no, my friends, Canada will be ruled by the good common sense of ordinary people, like all of us here today."

He finished with a wave of his hat. Some were embarrassed by his words, for these were plain people, not used to talking about what was most important to them. But there was wild clapping and cheering from others.

Just as the noise was dying down, someone pointed to a buggy coming at breakneck speed up the road. The horse pulling the buggy was dripping white lather off its flanks. It skidded to a halt, in front of the crowd. There were two people in the buggy. Fridbjorn Jonsson was driving, and beside him was a heavily veiled woman, dressed all in black. She raised the veil from her face, tucked it up on the brim of her hat and looked around. Maggie looked at Mother, and Mother looked at Maggie and shrugged. "I've never seen her before," she said.

Just then, a boy broke from the crowd and ran toward the buggy. "Mum!" Nicholas shouted. "It's me mum!"

Chapter Twenty-Five

Coming Home

The next half-hour was a jumble of explanations. Nicholas'
mother looked pale and tired. She told them how happy she
had been when Miss Charity showed her Mr. Jonsson's letter
asking her to start a dressmaking shop in Valhalla. She had
immediately written to say that she was feeling a little better
and that Miss Charity had offered to bring her with her next
load of boys and girls to Canada.

She said she had thought of nothing but being reunited
with her son on the long journey to Manitoba and it never
entered her mind that she might arrive before her letter did.
Only when she had alighted from the train in Valhalla did she
find out that her son lived several miles away, and she had no
way of getting to him. Luckily she was able to find Mr.
Jonsson, who knew of the picnic and brought her here at top
speed, afraid they would arrive after everyone had gone home.

Unless her son had other plans, she said, Nicholas would
come with her back to Valhalla this very evening. Mr. Jonsson
said there were a few sticks of furniture in the rooms above his
shop, enough for her and Nicholas to set up housekeeping.

"Well, Newt," said Pa to Mr. Ebenezer, "it looks like you just lost your hired man."

Nicholas had been standing quietly, listening to his mother talk, smiling a little. Now he moved to stand by Pa, facing Newt Ebenezer.

"I'll go with me mum now, but I'll come back in a few days to pick up m' trunk. And when I come, I'll pick up m' pay."

"Your what?" spluttered Newt, his face getting red.

"M' pay. You agreed with Miss Charity that I should get two dollars a month for doing the farm work. You owe me twenty dollars."

"Twenty dollars!" gasped Newt. "Now where would I get that kind of money?"

"How about looking in your pocket?" asked a quiet voice. Maggie was astonished to realize it was Matilda Ebenezer talking. "You got that money for selling those hogs, Newt. The boy worked hard for his pay. It's only right he gets what we owe him."

Newt Ebenezer looked cornered. His pale eyes darted around, seeking a means of escape. Everyone held their breath, then Nicholas, Pa and Mr. Trent all took a step toward him. Finally he raised his hands and laughed in a forced way.

"Take it easy, take it easy. No one can say Newt Ebenezer doesn't pay his debts." He put his hand in his pocket, pulled out some wrinkled bills, counted out twenty dollars and handed it to Nicholas. Then, without speaking, he turned and walked away. Matilda hurried after him, reaching for his sleeve.

Mother took Nicholas' mum to the table to get her some supper; Mr. Phillips-Jones rode past them at a gallop, heading for home. Maggie spotted Miss Fieldmont and Mr. Trent on the veranda. They were talking very seriously, then they were silent, and Mr. Trent took the teacher's hand in his and kissed it.

Maggie felt she couldn't take any more happiness in one day. She asked Nicholas if he would like to go for a ride on the prairie.

They let Penny and Copper have their heads and they cantered for a while before they realized where they were going. Then they pulled up near the creek, looking down at the tangle of willows along its edge, and the water gleaming through gaps in the branches. Saskatoon bushes were growing here and there among the willows. Their branches were hanging low with plump red berries. Mother had said just yesterday that the saskatoons would be blue and ripe in a couple of weeks and they must pick all they could for they made the sweetest pies of any.

While Maggie was thinking this, a strange noise intruded on her consciousness. At first, it seemed to be an unidentifiable rumbling, then it changed, and she thought it was the creek rushing and splashing. Then she saw it.

There, hanging from a cloud over the creek, was a waterfall, the bright prairie sunlight winking and glinting off its face.

Both she and Nicholas knew instantly what was happening. It was time for her to go back to her own home, her own time, her own life. She didn't want to go. She wanted to stay with Mother and Pa. They were her parents now. She wanted to see Nicholas and his mother build a home for themselves in this young country. She wanted to go to school in Valhalla with Kristjana. She wanted to see Crocus grow into a fine, strong workhorse. What if I just ride away? she thought. What would happen then?

At this moment, something happened that was even more strange than the sudden appearance of the waterfall. A slight girl with long brown hair stepped out from the falls. She was dressed in a faded green print dress. The dress was dry, absolutely dry. Maggie's heart thudded in her chest. For she knew that the girl stepping out from the falls was Ellie — the real Ellie Trenholme.

Chapter Twenty-Six

The Waterfall

*E*llie looked around her in amazement. "Oh! The creek," was all she said, her voice cracking with emotion. Then she turned to Maggie and Nicholas.

They slipped to the ground from Penny's and Copper's backs and stood, side by side. Maggie stepped forward. "Yes, you've come home," she said simply. "My name is Maggie. I've been living here, taking your place while you've been gone." Then she remembered her manners. "And this is Nicholas Camper. He's from England. He'll be a good friend."

For she knew at once she couldn't stay. Not now that Ellie was back. She had to go back to her own time to make room for Ellie.

"While I've been away?" said Ellie. "But I've only been gone a few minutes."

Nicholas and Maggie stared at her, confused. Then the light dawned in Maggie's face.

"I think I know what's happened. You went into the waterfall and came out somewhere else. Is that right?"

"Yes," said Ellie. "I went into the waterfall and came out in a strange country. It had high hills covered with trees, and there was a deep ravine. The waterfall was falling into that ravine. I was frightened, so I walked right back into the falls, and here I am at home." She looked around her, still with a puzzled look. "But it's summer time. A few minutes ago, when I went into the falls, it was autumn."

"I think I can explain," said Maggie. "You didn't just travel to a different place, but to a different time. I'm sure of it. You didn't stay long enough to find out, but you travelled to the future."

"It sounds odd, but then odd things have happened," said Ellie. Then she turned and looked thoughtfully at the falls hanging over the creek. When she turned back to Maggie, she said simply, "Tell me more."

"I've time-travelled twice now — once through the falls, and last year through a whirlpool," said Maggie. "As far as I can figure out, time stops on the other side, in modern times, but times passes normally on this side, in olden times."

They began walking, the horses following on loose reins, sometimes dropping their heads to snatch a mouthful of grass. They reached the spot where Ellie's grandpa was buried. The summer grasses had grown high, hiding the headstone. But they all knew it was there, a part of the prairies, just as Grandpa's spirit was.

"Why?" asked Maggie. "Do you know why I came to take your place?"

Ellie looked thoughtful. "When did you come?"

"In September, just before school opened."

"That's when Bill Bristol's gang kidnapped me. They held me for weeks in a cave they had dug. They didn't hurt me, but they were going to if I hadn't escaped. I heard them — they were ready to kill me." She thought for a moment, then her face brightened. "You're the girl who set me free, aren't you? You saved my life!"

"Where did you go that day after we separated?" asked Maggie. "I watched for you for weeks. I was sure you would come home."

"It's not very clear in my mind," said Ellie vaguely. "But I do remember running and running through the trees and hearing the sound of someone chasing me. I was out of breath, ready to give up, when suddenly there was this waterfall in front of me. I'd never seen anything like it before. I thought waterfalls were only in books. I could hear the hooves of the horse and the man shouting; then I could hear the breath of the horse; then, somehow, I was inside that waterfall. When I came out, I was in that strange country."

"I think the waterfall was there for me," said Maggie, "and the wrong girl ran into it by accident."

Ellie gazed across the prairie. Orange lilies studded the long grass. Wild rose bushes were pink with blossoms. "Oh my!" she said quietly. "It's so good to be home."

"You can't tell anyone else that," said Maggie. "Nobody knows you've been away. Mother and Pa are over at the Dominion Day picnic. You can ride back there with Nicholas. But first we've got to go back to the house to change clothes."

Maggie and Ellie rode Penny and Nicholas rode Copper, back to the little log house that Maggie had learned to love. Nicholas stayed with the horses while the girls went inside. In the lean-to, Ellie slipped out of her dress and into the pink dress Maggie had worn to the picnic. Ellie put the green dress into the clothes-box.

"It's last year's dress, so Mother won't be surprised if she finds it," she explained when Maggie looked doubtful.

Then Maggie put on her jeans, tee-shirt, socks and sneakers. Ellie was intrigued by the strange costume, and Maggie had to tell some more of her own story.

"I'm glad to meet you," said Ellie, "even if it is only for a little while. Nobody else would ever believe our stories."

"I think some will believe," said Maggie. "I think real true friends will believe. Nicholas believes. You'll know when the time comes who you can tell."

Then she thought of seeing Colleen again, soon, and she started to feel excited. "There's someone in my own time that I can tell," she said. "She thinks I don't want to be her real true friend because I wouldn't confide in her. That's something I've learned here — I learned from Mother that you have to be honest and show your feelings for those you care for."

"You learned that from Mother?" asked Ellie incredulously.

Then Maggie told Ellie about Christmas Day and how close Mother had come to saying she loved her. She went on explaining things. "You have a lot of geometry and Latin to learn so you can write the entrance examination for Valhalla School," she said. "If you work hard, I think you'll be able to pass. It's only July and you can study while you're herding cows. Miss Fieldmont will answer your questions. She's a very good teacher."

There was so much more she wanted to say on the ride back to the creek. So much had happened since she had come to Manitoba. But, there was the waterfall, shimmering in the afternoon sun, waiting for her.

"Don't worry," said Nicholas, guessing what she was thinking. "On our way back to the picnic, I'll tell the new Ellie about what's been happening."

"I think she's the old Ellie," said Maggie. They all laughed, then they stopped suddenly, for they were overcome by the wonder of it all.

The girls slid off Penny's back to the ground and stood silently for a moment. Then Ellie opened her arms and they hugged each other. "Thank you," Ellie whispered. "How can I thank you for saving my life?" Then she walked downstream a little way and waited. Maggie knew she was giving her some time alone with Nicholas.

Nicholas jumped off Copper's back, and both chestnuts ambled closer to the creek and began grazing. The boy stood with his head bowed. "I'm glad you came to my time," he said. "Without you as me friend, I'd've gone starkers at the Ebenezers'. I owe you so much. You taught me to read and ride your horses. You took me to town so I met Mr. Jonsson. You kept me from giving up."

"No, Nicholas," said Maggie firmly. "All those good things happened because you are so brave and smart. Mr. Jonsson would never have asked you to be his apprentice just because you're my friend. You convinced him how much you wanted to follow in your father's footsteps, and how hard you were willing to work to do that."

"I don't think it would've worked out without you," said Nicholas stubbornly.

Without realizing it, as they talked they had been walking toward the waterfall, and once again its roaring filled their ears.

"I think I have to go, now, Nicholas," said Maggie sadly. "I don't have any choice, anymore than when I came here."

"Don't forget us," said Nicholas. He reached out toward her, then, suddenly shy, he dropped his hand to his side.

"Never," said Maggie. She looked behind her across the prairie to the Trenholmes' house, the windows shining in the slanting rays of the sun. "I'll never forget any of you."

She went to Ellie's horses. She rubbed Copper between his eyes, then she put her arm around Penny's head and laid her cheek against the filly's velvet muzzle.

She spoke only once more. "I know Ellie will take good care of Penny and Copper. And I'll bet she'd be happy if you come out and ride them sometimes."

She looked at Nicholas, but her eyes were blurred with tears, so she couldn't see him clearly. Then she stepped through the shining wall of water and was gone.

· · ·

Maggie was caught in the force of the falls; then she was pushed through the wall of water and was, once again, on dry ground. She knew at once she was home in New Brunswick, in the chasm deep in the forest, the waterfall splashing behind her. She automatically checked her watch, then she checked the position of the sun and realized that no time had passed while she'd been away.

She followed the path, up the side of the chasm, and sat down on a fallen tree. She needed time to think, to try to get things into perspective. The roaring and splashing of the falls was still surrounding her. Somehow, she felt, as long as the noise was so intense, she was still connected with that other world.

The other world that she didn't want to leave. Her stomach twisted with pain. It was the same pain she had felt when she first arrived in Manitoba, and she knew what it was. Home-sickness.

Then she smiled through her tears. She would never understand the magic, but she knew she had done something wonderful while she lived in the past. She loved Pa and Mother very much, and she could comfort herself with the knowledge that she had spared them unimaginable sorrow. She had given them back their daughter.

Finally, the girl with the long brown hair stood up and brushed her cheeks dry. It was time to start the trek back to the car. If she was late, Aunt Kate would be anxious. Maggie didn't want to worry her. Maggie understood her great-aunt well enough to know how much the old lady needed her. Aunt Kate needed Maggie's optimism and enthusiasm because she had none of her own.

When Maggie reached the car, Aunt Kate checked her watch. "We were beginning to think you'd never come," she said grumpily.

Maggie climbed into the back seat, beside Colleen. Colleen was reading her book and refused to look up. Maggie knew she had deeply hurt someone who meant a great deal to her.

Maggie reached over and put her hand over the text, forcing Colleen to look at her. "When we get home, let's take our bikes for a ride along the river," she said. Then she dropped her voice to a whisper. "I'm sorry for shutting you out. I promise I won't do it again. You're my best friend in the world, and I need to talk. I've got such a lot of things to tell you!"

. . .

All summer, while they rode their bikes and canoed and walked on the riverbank, Colleen asked Maggie questions about her experiences in the past. Maggie was surprised and delighted with her interest, for she didn't want to forget one detail of what had happened.

One day Colleen said, "Don't you care about what happened to them?"

"What do you mean?" asked Maggie.

"All those people you lived with while you were — away. I'll bet you could find out about them. It was just a little over a hundred years ago. There are history books and things. I'll bet you could find out."

So the girls went to the library and asked for information about Manitoba pioneers for a project they were working on.

The librarian took the details and said she would see if she could get a book on loan from Manitoba. A few weeks later, she phoned to say it had arrived.

The book was a large volume, printed in 1989, called *Remembering the Pioneers — The History of Valhalla, Manitoba.* Inside were the stories of all the pioneer families who had settled in Valhalla and surrounding school districts.

Maggie's hands were shaking so hard that Colleen had to take the book from her. The first name they found was Camper. There was a wedding picture of a young couple in old-fashioned clothes. Under the picture it said this was Nicholas Camper and his bride, Kristjana Jonsson. He had worked in Valhalla as a boot and harness maker for many years, greatly admired for his skill. She was a founding member of the Valhalla Suffrage Society which was credited with helping to make Manitoba the first province in Canada to give women the vote. The couple lived into their eighties. They had two children, a boy named Nicholas who became a doctor, and a girl named Sigridur who became a writer and lecturer.

Maggie felt her eyes swimming when she looked at that picture. Nicholas looked so proud, and Kristjana's happy smile shone from the page.

She held her breath as they flipped through the pages, looking for Trenholme. There was no picture here, but there was a story about Pa and Mother and their long life in Victoria School District. Their daughter, Elinor, had married a man named Jonathan Staples. The couple lived in Prairie Mound, where they raised horses for farms. In later years, when horses were replaced by machines, they raised horses for pleasure-riding. They showed their animals at fairs and exhibitions all over Western Canada, and won many prizes and awards. They had a family of four girls and three boys. One of their daughters had written the piece and she ended by saying, "I remember my parents best for their kind and loving ways. We were very lucky in that we had a warm and happy family life."

Long after Colleen went home, Maggie read those words over and over — "a warm and happy family life." The life ahead of her would likely turn out to be totally different from Ellie's, just as her life now was totally different. But for one shining moment, their two lives had converged, and Ellie had given Maggie as great a gift as Maggie had given her.

Explosion at Dawson Creek

Travelling by train to Montreal for a summer holiday, Maggie and Marc take another trip back in time and mysteriously arrive at Dawson Creek, British Columbia during the Second World War. Construction of the Alaska highway has started and Dawson Creek, known in present day as "mile zero" of the Alaska Highway, is a boom town.

Mysterious nighttime activities and a near-escape from arrest by American soldiers keep them on their toes and curious about their new life. Where does Maggie's boss go every night? What happens to their friends when fire starts a dynamite blast in town? And will they we able to return to their own time?

"Author Elaine Breault Hammond's deft writing proves that you don't need towering icebergs or castles full of noble knights to create an engrossing time-travel story."

—*Owl Canadian Family*

ISBN 0-921556-75-6   **$7.95**

Time-Travel Adventures
by Elaine Breault Hammond

The Secret Under the Whirlpool

Maggie is spending the loneliest summer holiday ever at her great-aunt's. Marc, her next door neighbour, is miserable because he is recovering from a car accident. Grudgingly they become friends and begin to explore their vacation island together. One day, while canoeing, they get caught in a storm. Without warning, they are drawn into a whirlpool that pulls them into a cave. The cave quickly fills up with water. Maggie and Marc fight for their lives. Suddenly, they find themselves on dry land in dense forest.

A monotonous summer vacation turns into an adventure of historic dimensions when Maggie and Marc travel back in time to eighteenth-century Acadia. Eventually, they must choose between living in the past or searching for a way home.

"A well-crafted adventure story ... Hammond writes with conviction, weaving history and fiction together seamlessly."
— *Atlantic Books Today*

"Excellent-quality historical fiction."
— *Books in Canada*

ISBN 0-921556-61-6 $7.95